Moving a respectable distance from the fiery blaze of the house, he laid Whitfield on the ground and was shocked to find that the man was still breathing.

From behind him someone said, "He went in after you, poor wretch."

Jesus, Clint thought, looking down at the man. Jesus Christ, what a waste.

"M—my daughter," Whitfield said hoarsely.

"Don't talk," Clint replied, shocked that the man could still do so.

"I—I must. Listen—please. There is a fortune ... waiting for her. There's a letter ... in my warbag ... a letter that will explain everything."

"Be quiet—"

The man's blackened hand came up and grabbed ahold of Clint's arm with surprising strength.

"Find her! Promise!"

"I promise."

The hand squeezed his arm tightly, then loosened its grip and fell to the ground.

Don't miss any of the lusty, hard-riding action in the Jove Western series, THE GUNSMITH

1. MACKLIN'S WOMEN
2. THE CHINESE GUNMEN
3. THE WOMAN HUNT
4. THE GUNS OF ABILENE
5. THREE GUNS FOR GLORY
6. LEADTOWN
7. THE LONGHORN WAR
8. QUANAH'S REVENGE
9. HEAVYWEIGHT GUN
10. NEW ORLEANS FIRE
11. ONE-HANDED GUN
12. THE CANADIAN PAYROLL
13. DRAW TO AN INSIDE DEATH
14. DEAD MAN'S HAND
15. BANDIT GOLD
16. BUCKSKINS AND SIX-GUNS
17. SILVER WAR
18. HIGH NOON AT LANCASTER
19. BANDIDO BLOOD
20. THE DODGE CITY GANG
21. SASQUATCH HUNT
22. BULLETS AND BALLOTS
23. THE RIVERBOAT GANG
24. KILLER GRIZZLY
25. NORTH OF THE BORDER
26. EAGLE'S GAP
27. CHINATOWN HELL
28. THE PANHANDLE SEARCH
29. WILDCAT ROUNDUP
30. THE PONDEROSA WAR
31. TROUBLE RIDES A FAST HORSE
32. DYNAMITE JUSTICE
33. THE POSSE
34. NIGHT OF THE GILA
35. THE BOUNTY WOMEN
36. BLACK PEARL SALOON
37. GUNDOWN IN PARADISE
38. KING OF THE BORDER
39. THE EL PASO SALT WAR
40. THE TEN PINES KILLER
41. HELL WITH A PISTOL
42. THE WYOMING CATTLE KILL
43. THE GOLDEN HORSEMAN
44. THE SCARLET GUN
45. NAVAHO DEVIL
46. WILD BILL'S GHOST
47. THE MINER'S SHOWDOWN
48. ARCHER'S REVENGE
49. SHOWDOWN IN RATON
50. WHEN LEGENDS MEET
51. DESERT HELL
52. THE DIAMOND GUN
53. DENVER DUO
54. HELL ON WHEELS
55. THE LEGEND MAKER
56. WALKING DEAD MAN
57. CROSSFIRE MOUNTAIN
58. THE DEADLY HEALER
59. THE TRAIL DRIVE WAR
60. GERONIMO'S TRAIL
61. THE COMSTOCK GOLD FRAUD
62. BOOM TOWN KILLER
63. TEXAS TRACKDOWN
64. THE FAST DRAW LEAGUE
65. SHOWDOWN IN RIO MALO
66. OUTLAW TRAIL
67. HOMESTEADER GUNS
68. FIVE CARD DEATH
69. TRAIL DRIVE TO MONTANA

And coming next month:
THE GUNSMITH #71: THE OLD WHISTLER GANG

TRIAL BY FIRE

J. R. ROBERTS

JOVE BOOKS, NEW YORK

THE GUNSMITH #70: TRIAL BY FIRE

A Jove Book / published by arrangement with
the author

PRINTING HISTORY
Jove edition / October 1987

All rights reserved.
Copyright © 1987 by Robert J. Randisi.
This book may not be reproduced in whole or in part,
by mimeograph or any other means, without permission.
For information address: The Berkley Publishing Group,
200 Madison Avenue, New York, New York 10016.

ISBN: 0-515-09258-4

Jove Books are published by The Berkley Publishing Group,
200 Madison Avenue, New York, New York 10016.
The name "JOVE" and the "J" logo
are trademarks belonging to Jove Publications, Inc.

PRINTED IN THE UNITED STATES OF AMERICA

10 9 8 7 6 5 4 3 2 1

ONE

Clint Adams slept as he rarely did. The mistress at the inn where he was staying had suggested a steaming cup of her own special home remedy—a brew that seemed to be part dynamite and part alkali—for the head cold and sore throat that had plagued him for the past week.

On his way up the stairs to his room Clint was stopped by the hunchbacked little man named Whitfield, who was also a guest. The man appeared out of the deep shadows created by the kerosene lamp Clint carried.

As usual, the thickset little man wore a tuniclike white shirt that helped conceal—to some extent, anyway—his swollen back. Thinning gray hair framed a broken face—a boxer's flat nose and thick lips—and dark eyes that seemed to look inward at some private sorrow. Other guests snickered about the little man and this was obviously the sort of treatment that Whitfield had long since become used to.

"So, she gave you her witch's brew, eh?"

Clint smiled, already feeling drowsy.

"She says it will help me sleep."

"Oh, it'll do that, all right," Whitfield said. There seemed to be more that the little man wanted to say, but he seemed apprehensive about saying it.

Clint held the lantern higher, the blue-yellow flame hissing in his hand.

"Mr. Adams, I—" Whitfield leaned closer.

"There's something I'd like to tell you, sir."

Clint smiled.

"I'll listen to anything you have to say, as long as you don't call me 'sir'."

The hunchback smiled. When he did that his face became pleasant looking—almost.

"All right."

"What do you want to tell me?"

Whitfield glanced up and down the darkened hallway.

"The mistress, she ain't as kindly as she seems."

"You've stayed here before, then?"

"Oh, many times, sin—uh, many times, and I've seen her give that brew to other people."

"Is it poison, or something?"

"No, not poison, but it does put a body 'deep in the lapp of Morpheus,' as my dear old Irish grandmother used to say."

"Really knocks you out, huh?"

"For hours."

Clint shrugged.

"I *could* use the sleep. This damn cold has really taken a lot out of me." Still, he thought, it wasn't wise for a man of his rep to sleep too soundly. Still, no one at this small, southern California stagecoach stop seemed to know who he was.

"Oh, the sleep will help you, of that there is no doubt, but—well, it wouldn't be hard for someone to rob a man who is in as deep a sleep as the mistress's brew puts him."

"It couldn't be all that deep," Clint said.

"Well, in any case, if you have anything of very real value—"

Clint put his hand on the hunchback's shoulder.

"I appreciate that advice, Mr. Whitfield, I really do."

TRIAL BY FIRE

Whitfield nodded, seemingly pleased at being called "mister." It had not happened often during his life—a life that had given him sixty years of little solace and much ridicule. Being a freak had not been easy work.

Whitfield went down the stairs, where laughter came from the bar where the mistress of the stagestop sang bawdy Gaelic songs and cheated guests at blackjack.

In his room Clint heeded the hunchback's warning by taking his saddlebags and stuffing them under his mattress. Although he doubted he would sleep so soundly that someone could enter his room, at least they wouldn't be able to take the saddlebags without waking him.

He took his modified Colt out of its holster and set it big and ready on the nightstand right next to the bed.

As it turned out, Whitfield had been right about at least one thing. The woman's brew put Clint to sleep almost immediately after he blew out the lamp, even before he could so much as remove his boots. He remembered starting to cough just before tumbling into a deep, black void . . .

The fire, which began in the kitchen, took less than five minutes to spread throughout the entire first floor and start its insidious way up the interior stairs.

Clint Adams, oblivious because of the concoction he'd imbibed, did not hear the fire that crackled loudly as it consumed timber or the smell of smoke that snaked beneath his door.

The fire raged—and Clint Adams slept on . . .

Behind the inn was a large rope corral where horses breathed silver in the frosty, brightly moonlit night. To the right of the inn stood two four-up Concord coaches, muddy, dusty, battered as they entered a new decade in which the iron horse would soon make them obsolete.

Corral and coaches alike were thrown into an eerie, hellish relief from the red-yellow flames that bloomed like an artificial sun. Horses neighed in fright; for a quarter mile the frost melted on the grass.

Near the inn, close as they could get, stood a wide circle of guests, some wrapped in blankets, some standing seemingly indifferent to the cold in nightshirts and other sleep wear.

The mistress of the place cried while men watched grim-faced. The flames had now seemed to claim the entire inn, casting an eerie yellow glow over their skin. Their eyes showed bitterness. You erected a few human symbols out here on the plains, but nature soon reminded you of her dominance. Nature took your possessions, your houses—nature even occasionally took your kin.

Whitfield was one of the men watching the flames but even in this moment of tragedy he was set apart from the others—as if his grief at this terrible spectacle was not worth hearing about. Even now you could see that the gaze of the others did not settle comfortably on the man's hunchback. Eyes soon moved on, uneasy—even, in a curious way, angry.

Whitfield was dressed only in trousers washed so many times that they had no exact color, his twisted torso wrapped in the familiar dirty tunic. He huddled into himself, his nose and knuckles frozen from the chill night, his eyes fixed on the timber of the roof that was now collapsing inward with a crash that shook the ground.

Then he realized what had been troubling him since the first calls of "Fire!" had roused him from his already uneasy sleep.

The man he'd been talking to earlier—Clint

TRIAL BY FIRE 5

Adams—the only person in the entire inn who did not look at him in disgust, was nowhere to be found.

Then Whitfield remembered the brew that the mistress had given him. Clint Adams was probably so deeply asleep that he had been unable to hear the warning shouts. By now, he would be overcome by the smoke.

"Mr. Adams is still in there!" Whitfield shouted to the others.

"If he's in there, he's a dead man now," one man replied aloud.

"But we've got to try and rescue him!" Whitfield said, moving toward the other men. He felt as always at such moments like a frustrated child in a world of adults—he was short, bent of stature, and without much strength. He had to depend on others to do for him the things he couldn't do.

The stagecoach driver, a grizzled man in an equally grizzled and worn hat, spat a stream of tobacco juice and grinned with brown teeth.

"Looks like you'll have to go in there and drag that feller out of there yerself."

The other men, grateful for the distraction, laughed along with the stage driver, thinking that was the funniest thing they'd ever heard.

"We can't just let him die!"

The stagecoach driver grinned again.

" 'Course we can."

Less than a minute later—thinking of how kindly Clint Adams had treated him—Whitfield ran toward the building, looking for the best way into the red-yellow inferno.

Behind him came the shouts of the others, calling him crazy, telling him to draw back, that the man inside must already be dead, but Whitfield couldn't really hear.

The flames crackled too loudly.

The timber falling was too deafening.

His heart was beating wildly in his ears.

The heat seemed to melt his skin even though he hadn't yet entered the hotel.

Then, gulping, he did what he knew he needed to do.

He ran into the blazing hotel.

TWO

If only by some form of self-preservation long perfected over the years, Clint Adams finally awoke and found himself in the center of a tightening circle of fire. He felt his hair singe, smelled it burn.

The brew the woman had given him, combined with the bad head cold, kept him from thinking with his usual clarity, or he might have simply rushed out. Instead, he paused to strap on his gun and remove his saddlebags from beneath the mattress. He was dressed, for he had fallen asleep that way. Above him he heard the timber of the roof crack from the pressure of the raging flames.

He knew he had only a second to flee the room.

Putting his forearm across his face, bending his head very low, he ran through the wall of heat and fire until he reached the hallway outside.

Then he saw the hunchbacked man.

Whitfield seemed to be completely enveloped in flame, his entire body nothing more than an eerie figure etched entirely in fire.

His screams could be heard above all else.

He came toward Clint, holding his arms forward as if in greeting.

Clint dove for him, ripping off his own shirt, throwing it over the face and torso of the little man and rolling him along the floor, trying to get the worst of the fire on the man's body extinguished.

Though the fire was finally extinguished Whitfield

was nothing more than a charred piece of meat, blackened flesh running with pus and blood.

The whites of his eyes were almost lurid in contrast with the coal color of his cheeks.

Clint picked the man up and found his way to the front stairs. Finding that they had already collapsed he reversed his course and hurried to the back stairs, where he was luckier. They were aflame, but still standing, and he hurried down them, knowing that they could give beneath his weight at any moment. Sure enough, as he reached the floor below, he heard a resounding crack as the stairway gave way. He hurried out the back door into the chilled night.

Moving a respectable distance from the fiery blaze of the house, he laid Whitfield on the ground and was shocked to find that the man was still breathing.

From behind him someone said, "He went in after you, poor wretch."

Jesus, Clint thought, looking down at the man. Jesus Christ, what a waste. This had happened to the man because he'd been trying to help Clint Adams, who had already been awake and on his way out.

"M—my daughter," Whitfield said hoarsely.

"Don't talk," Clint replied, shocked that the man could still do so.

"I—I must. Listen—please." There was so much pain in the man's voice that Clint winced. "There is a fortune . . . waiting for her. There's a letter . . . in my warbag . . . a letter that will explain everything."

"Be quiet—"

The man's blackened hand came up and grabbed ahold of Clint's arm with surprising strength.

"Find her! Promise!"

"I promise."

The hand squeezed his arm tightly, then loosened its grip and fell to the ground.

TRIAL BY FIRE 9

• • •

"I'll be taking that now."

Clint held his hand out for the proprietress of the inn to place the hunchback's warbag in.

"Why should I give it to you?" she demanded.

"Because if you don't, I'm going to have to take it from you. I don't want to have to do that unless it's absolutely necessary."

"Oh," she said sardonically, "a real gentleman."

Clint kept his hand out, waiting.

It was now near dawn, three hours after he'd run to safety carrying the little hunchback, Whitfield.

He'd found a place on a small hillock, under an elm, and had wrapped Whitfield up and left him until another stage came along to transport the body to the nearest town for a decent burial.

He'd had less success with the innkeeper.

A shrewd woman, she had gone through the belongings of all three people who had been burned in the blaze. She'd managed to keep two of the bags. The third one, Whitfield's, Clint now demanded.

They stood near the rope corral. The horses glistened with dew. Their breath was an icy blue color. To the east of the corral stood Clint's wagon and his own horses, including Duke, his prize black gelding. Clint wanted nothing better than to get moving.

But first, this.

"I'd oblige the man, Maude," said a white-haired man in a black frock coat who had just wandered from the big Conestoga wagon where the survivors were getting up breakfast. "Him and that hunchback sort of became friends. It's only fitting that this'n here take the hunchback's bag."

"Some husband you are."

Clint felt immediate pity for the man.

"We got plenty of loot, Maude. That plump little

woman with the colored red hair left enough jewels behind. Besides, I'd hate to see this young gentleman shoot you. I'm too old to be gettin' myself a new wife."

Maude said to Clint, "Mister, you can kiss my ass seven ways from sundown."

But in the end she gave it to him and ten minutes later Clint's wagon was a silhouette against a purple morning sky.

THREE

Five days later Clint rolled his wagon down the edge of a mountain pass that led to the city of Chalmers, California. It was a small city that boasted a four-block shopping section, and was probably heavily supported by the sawmill that was nearly as formidable as some of the factories he'd seen on trips back East.

The time was high noon and the day was Sunday. If Clint needed a reminder of that, church bells sounded off, seeming to echo off the blue-tipped mountains that ringed the valley.

Clint moved further into the town, mindful of the fact that he still had Whitfield's letter in his pocket.

A sign announced: CHALMERS: 1/2 MILE. STRANGERS WELCOME. He started past the sign when he saw a buggy coming toward him on the stage road.

Two white-haired old ladies in church bonnets were tucked inside the buggy behind the aged farm horse that pulled them. A plaid blanket was thrown over their legs out of deference to the crisp day.

Clint pulled his wagon over and tipped his hat.

"Good day, ladies."

"Good day yourself, stranger," the one holding the reins said. This close, it was easy to see that they were sisters. They were probably in their sixties.

"I wonder if you ladies could help me," Clint said.

"We would certainly be willing to try, young man."

Clint waved the letter—Whitfield's letter—and

said, "I wonder if you might be able to tell me where the Pratt House is located?"

The sisters, without hesitation, glanced at each other as if Clint had suggested some truly filthy sexual act.

"It burned," said the one with the reins.

"What?"

"It burned down."

"The Pratt House burned?"

"To the ground, I'm happy to report," said the same sister. She wore a red bonnet, and her sister a blue one. They were both as prim as deacons talking about the evils of whiskey.

"Where was this place, anyway?"

The one with the blue bonnet pointed west.

"About a mile or so that way."

"How did it come to burn down?"

"The God-fearing folks of this town took it upon themselves—one night when the Lord spoke in a particularly loud voice—to bring torches into the darkness and incinerate till not a single brick stood upright." This was the red-bonneted lady, speaking with an odd sense of pride. Clint wondered if she and her sister were right there holding torches.

"Seems to me that's just the opposite of how real God-fearing folks would act."

"Are you saying that we are . . . heathens?" asked the blue-bonneted sister.

"I'm saying that, at the very least, you're a little rambunctious."

The two women flushed.

"Now he has built a new place," said the sister with the reins and the blue bonnet.

"Who's built a new place?"

"Why, Dr. Vernon, of course. Lucifer's voice on this earth."

"Where would I find this Dr. Vernon?"

The red-bonneted lady pointed west again.

"About two miles southwest of his old house. That's where you'll find him, practicing his sinful ways."

The other one smiled.

"But he won't be there for long."

Clint smiled back.

"Another get-together by the God-fearing folks of the town?"

"Exactly."

"I'm beginning to have doubts about what that sign there says," Clint said, inclining his head toward the wooden sign.

"What sign?"

"Strangers welcome."

With that he moved on, tipping his hat to the two God-fearing little old ladies.

Reaching the sight of what had once been the Pratt House, Clint could see that the God-fearing folks of Chalmers had done themselves proud. Where there had once been a vast stone wall there was now rubble. Where there had once been proud columns there were now only smoke-blackened stubs. For fifty yards around the burned-out hull the grass no longer grew.

It all looked very familiar.

Clint took the letter out of his pocket and read it again.

My Darling Daughter,

You have never met me. I fled St. Louis just before your birth. Owing to a deformity of mine your mother was ashamed for people to know who had fathered her child.

In my time since then I have been a thief and a beggar, a cheat and a drunkard. One night I was on a stagecoach with a travelling diamond merchant, when another passenger drew a gun and shot both the merchant and me. A few moments later he shot the driver. Both the merchant and the driver died, but I was not nearly as dead as I pretended.

As the thief took from the merchant a cache of diamonds, I grabbed his gun and shot him. I am ashamed to admit that I reported none of this. I took the fortune in diamonds and fled.

I hid most of the diamonds, using only some of them to get enough money to track you down. I finally found that you were staying at the Pratt House, run by Dr. John Vernon. I also learned that the Pratt House was a place for the insane. I blame myself and my desertion of you for your having ended up there.

Several times I rode the winding path to the Pratt House, but I could never bring myself to knock at the door. Instead, I write you this letter, to tell you where the diamonds are hidden. Think back to an expression your mother certainly used with you, "The steps leading to the Lord's house," and you will know where I hid them.

One day you will surely leave that place, and I plan to leave this letter where you will get it.

I am too cowardly to ever see you myself, daughter, but know that I love you, and have provided for you.

Love,
Father.

Clint had just folded the letter and put it back in his pocket when he heard the unmistakable sound of a hammer of a handgun or rifle being cocked—most likely, from his experience, a rifle.

A male voice said, "Turn around real slow, mister, and hand me that letter."

FOUR

Clint turned in his seat, tucking the letter away and looked at the owner of the voice. The man, dapper in an Edwardian coat, with a black homburg angled rakishly atop his head, much resembled a funeral director—and, as far as Clint was concerned, he might as well have been.

"Can I help you?" Clint asked.

"What are you doing here?"

"I might ask you the same thing."

"I am asking you, sir."

The man rode around to the front of Clint's wagon, stopping his horse next to Clint's team. That was all the opportunity that Clint needed. He yanked back on the reins and the horses reared up, causing the stranger's mount to do the same. Clint was down on the ground in a second and had the man's rifle by the barrel. He yanked it from the man's hand, and then pulled the man down off his horse.

When the man had regained his feet Clint grabbed the front of his fancy coat, spun him around, and hurled him hard against a tree.

"I'm not real partial to people who come up from behind me with guns, mister," Clint said between his teeth. His anger was just barely concealed.

If the Gunsmith had a single fear, it was being shot in the back—as his friend Bill Hickok had been—and this fella could have done just that. It was all Clint could do to keep from slapping the man's face raw.

"I—I was afraid that you would shoot if I didn't threaten you with my weapon."

"Why would I want to shoot you?"

"I thought that perhaps you were one of the townspeople," the man said nervously, "one of the people who burned me out last time."

Up close the man's cheeks were as cadaverous as Abraham Lincoln's himself, but he carried nothing of the former President's grace and poise.

"You're Dr. Vernon?"

"I am."

"Why were you so interested in seeing my letter?"

"I thought that perhaps it was something of mine that you had recovered from the rubble."

"Well, it isn't," Clint said. "It belongs to me."

"I—I'm sorry for all of this," the man said. "It's just that after all of the trouble I've had here the past few years—" From the inside pocket of his jacket he took a big silver Ingram watch and consulted it. "I really think I had better get back to my institute. I try never to be gone for too long. This has all been a terrible misunderstanding."

The doctor moved away from the tree experimentally, and when Clint did not try to stop him the man relaxed visibly, taking a deep breath.

"Perhaps you would like to join me for dinner at the institute," Vernon suggested, "so that I may make amends in some small way?"

Clint thought about the letter, and about finding Whitfield's daughter, who was apparently one of Dr. Vernon's patients and decided that having dinner with the good doctor was a fine idea.

"I'd be happy to join you for dinner, Doctor."

"Excellent. It will take you longer to get there with your wagon and all, so I will ride ahead and have a place set for you when you arrive."

There was a brief moment of suspicion, but Clint felt safe in disregarding it.

"Fine."

TRIAL BY FIRE

Looking at the rifle in Clint's hand the doctor asked, "Uh, may I have . . ."

Clint looked at the rifle, and then at the doctor, and decided it was safe to return the weapon.

He handed it to the doctor, who accepted it and pointed it at the ground.

"Again, I apologize for coming up behind you that way. I hope dinner will in some small way make up for it."

"I'm sure it will, Doctor."

The doctor rode ahead after giving Clint specific instructions on how to get to his "institute."

Was that what they were calling homes for the insane these days?

The place was a rambling stone structure set against hills beautiful with autumn. To the east of the institute, several acres of corn had been planted. To the west black and white dairy cattle roamed a hillside, lazing in the sparse grass or drinking from the thin, winding stream. Sunlight played off the institute's window like liquid gold. The entire scene would have been idyllic except for the black iron bars on the third-floor windows.

A dirt road wound through oaks and elms and emerged on a plain leading directly to the institute. It was in the middle of the road that Clint saw the tiny bald man with the broom he was obviously using as a horse, the way children did when they imitated the cowboys they read about in dime novels.

"Whoa, whoa," the man said to the broom. Then he made fat, moist horsey noises with his mouth.

"When I run too hard," he said to Clint, "he gets very tired."

"I can see that."

"I'm Elmer."

"Hello, Elmer. I'm Clint."

"I wish I had a horse like yours."

Elmer was talking about Duke.

"He is beautiful, isn't he?" Clint said.

"He sure is."

Elmer wore a much-washed, loose-fitting shirt and pants with a piece of twine for a belt.

"You here to see Doc Vernon?"

"Yes, I am."

"He's good to me."

"I'm sure he is."

"My ma, she used to keep me in this shed and let my brothers beat me sometimes."

"I'm sorry, Elmer. That wasn't very nice of her."

"Doc Vernon heard about it and then made the sheriff bring me to him. I like it here a lot better."

"I'm sure it's a very nice place, Elmer."

The conversation was melancholy enough—with its images of hostile mothers and malevolent brothers—but it was even worse when you looked closely at the dried skin and wrinkles on Elmer's face and realized that the man had to be in his fifties now. The incidents he was describing had to have happened many years before, yet to him they seemed fresh, recent.

"Doc Vernon, he says I can't help the way I am."

Clint nodded to Elmer's broom and said, "Tell you what, Elmer. How'd you like to ride alongside my wagon up to the institute. It's almost dinnertime."

Elmer grinned.

"That would be fun."

"Well, come on then. Let's get going."

"You're a nice man."

"That's what they tell me."

Clint urged his team forward slowly, so Elmer could keep up, and patiently fielded all of the man's questions. It was like dealing with a remarkably inquisitive four-year-old. He liked the little man—but at the same time was exhausted by his questions.

FIVE

The shadows reminded her of night, and night was her only friend.

She wished there was someplace between living (which frightened her) and dying (which frightened her even more) where you just drifted in silence and shadow, alone and safe . . .

She had not awakened until half an hour ago, long after decent people—

She smiled to herself at that thought.

Decent people.

As if she could ever be decent people.

She sat in the corner, in the rocking chair, pretending to herself that last night had not happened.

Next to the door across from her the umbrella was propped. A very ordinary-looking umbrella, used against the sun and the rain. Dark blue, made of silk.

Only when you manipulated the handle a certain way did you realize that this was a very special umbrella.

You pressed a small button with your thumb and the handle pulled away from the rest of it—

—and you held a two-foot dagger in your hand.

She sighed and returned to staring at the dust floating like tiny, drifting particles of gold through the light.

The umbrella . . .

. . . memories of last night: fog, the glistening, dew-covered plank sidewalks that stank of wet pine, the dying smell of leaves having been burned earlier in the evening, the clip-clop of horses pulling the carriages of the wealthy, the nimbus of the corner lamplights like fading beacons, the distant laughter of taverns and the bright cheap laughter of whores, and then the man emerging from the alleyway . . .

. . . and the man saying, "Hello, dearie, are you doing anything this evening?"

And she would have been all right if he hadn't reached out and grabbed her sleeve and pulled her drunkenly to him. Doing as she had prayed she would never do again—and if *that* were true, why keep the umbrella?—she pressed the button and felt the dagger slide from the umbrella's shaft . . .

. . . there in the fog the man stiffened and slid to the alley floor, hands slick with his own blood, and then she passed on, feeling oddly elated . . .

So now she waited for the shadows in the room to lengthen and deepen.

For the peace and safety of the shadows.

Of night itself . . .

After a time, the practical side of her nature taking over, she got up from the rocker and went over to the umbrella and carried it to the porcelain washing bowl and proceeded to clean it thoroughly.

Some of the blood had dried and was now litle more than a dusty powder.

But the tip—

The tip was still sticky with blood and flecks of something else from the man's innards, and that made it real, brought it home again . . .

She threw herself down on the bed and cried, not for the dead man, but for herself, her face in her hands . . .

She was scarcely aware of the knock at the door.

"Miss?"

It was the woman who owned the boardinghouse.

She cleared her throat, trying to sound perfectly normal in reply.

"Yes?"

TRIAL BY FIRE 21

"There's good roast beef and cherry pie for dinner. Won't you come down and join us?"

"I'm afraid I'm not—not feeling well."

"Again? I worry about you, miss. I surely do."

"I appreciate that."

"Well, I'll be saving you some dinner. Whenever you get hungry—"

"That's very kind of you."

"You're a nice lady, miss. It's my pleasure."

The sound of retreating footsteps along the corridor, down the steps.

The sound of carriages in the street outside. Children laughing on what was probably the last Indian summer Sunday of the year.

She lay back on the bed and pressed her face deep into the bed, thinking about Dr. Vernon, creating her own shadows and trying to forget the incident of the previous night, in the fog, and the easy way the dagger had slid from the umbrella into her hand . . .

SIX

The Pratt Institute smelled of homebaked bread and beef stew, noticeable even from the outside. Those odors came through several mullioned windows that were open to absorb late afternoon sunlight.

Clint had pulled the wagon up next to the east end of the long stone building, with the dairy cattle roaming the hills directly behind, with the creek winding silver through the brown autumn grass, and stepped down and permitted himself to inhale the pure, good smells of the moment.

Dr. Vernon was waiting for him at the front door. Clint approached with Elmer right behind him.

"I see you've met Elmer."

Elmer grinned at Dr. Vernon and said, "We're friends, Doctor."

"I'm sure you are, Elmer," Vernon said, smiling a benign smile. "Why don't you go and . . . put your mount away. Dinner is almost ready."

"Yes, Doctor." Elmer looked at Clint with a great, wide smile and said, "See you later, friend."

"See you later, Elmer."

"I'll have someone see to your horses and wagon," Vernon promised Clint. "Please, come inside."

Vernon's frock coat was gone. Now he wore just a somewhat soiled shirt with an open celluloid collar and a dark brocaded vest. With his widow's peak and melancholy gaze, he still reminded Clint of Abe Lincoln.

"This is quite a place," Clint said.

"Only place like it in the West," Vernon said. He smiled and said, "You'll forgive my show of pride."

"Seems you've got something here to be proud of."

Vernon's dark eyes shone with zeal.

"Actually, I do. Do you know anything about how so-called 'madmen' are treated?"

Clint shrugged.

"From what I gather, they don't exactly enjoy what you'd call a wonderful life."

"You have a nice, ironic way of putting things."

"I didn't mean—"

"No, no, there was no offense taken. It's true, in most institutions, they do not have very happy lives. I am trying to change that here."

As they walked through the halls, Vernon gave Clint a quick description of how "lunatics" were treated.

Many of them were shackled or chained in dark parts of houses or basements and fed and cared for by family members, the way you would care for a pet. These were the more fortunate ones. Others were left to wander, begging for food. Those who could not find sustenance starved to death—or, in many cases, were shot or beaten by townspeople who saw them as being possessed by demons.

Then there were the so-called "hospitals," which, according to the windbag state legislators that funded the places, were supposedly "enlightened" havens for the insane and retarded.

According to Dr. Vernon, however, this was not the case at all.

Every sort of barbaric treatment was inflicted on the poor inmates of these places—from treatment with enemas to bloodletting and beatings. In the case of young women, there were rapes by guards and other inmates. Only gradually was the medical establishment beginning to see that their "treatment" of the

TRIAL BY FIRE

insane was inhuman and outdated.

"But things aren't happening fast enough to effect the sort of change we truly need," Vernon said. "My father was the owner of several railroads, Mr. Adams. He died in the Andes, when he was mountain climbing with one of President Grant's favorite drinking partners." He wiped a lock of sweaty black hair away from his forehead, where it had become stuck. "I took my inheritance and went to Europe where I studied both medicine and mesmerism."

"Hypnotism?"

"Yes, that is another word for it. You understand what it is?"

"Not very well. I've read about it, but my knowledge beyond that . . ."

Vernon explained.

Franz Anton Mesmer discovered the process in 1775 and began to apply it to healing both physical and mental ailments—but it was then discovered by the same medical investigative committee that had funded Mesmer in the first place.

"That didn't stop succeeding generations of medical people from applying *his* techniques and methods—with great success."

"So that's what your institute is all about?"

"Precisely. The curative powers of mesmerism—or hypnotism, if you prefer. Perhaps, while you are here, I can demonstrate for you."

"After dinner."

The doctor smiled and said, "But of course. After dinner."

SEVEN

Darkness.
She lay on the bed.
Watching the very last of the light becoming . . .
Darkness.
Behind the curtain.
Night.
She got up from the bed and walked to the dresser with the pitcher and bowl on it. She poured water into the pitcher, then stripped off all of her clothes. Naked, she ran her hands over her body, starting between her legs, up over her torso—pausing to cup her breasts—and then ran her fingers through her hair.

She needed to wash her hair.
And her bountiful breasts.
And perfume the tender moist lips between her legs.
In her head, the voice spoke to her—
Tonight, it said . . .
Tonight . . .
Again . . .
Somewhere over there in the darkness, the umbrella beckoned to her—
The very special umbrella.
Ready.
Once again.
For tonight.

EIGHT

Over a hot and tasty dinner of stew and big chunks of bread covered with fresh butter, Clint heard the rest of the doctor's story.

Despite the fact that through simple medical practices coupled with mesmerism Vernon had begun to help many insane and retarded people, a certain vocal faction in the neighboring town of Chalmers persisted in seeing the doctor and his work as being inspired by the devil.

"Religious fanatics!"

So one night a dozen or so men in white robes and cowls ringed the institute with torches in their hands and set it on fire.

Loss of the building was bad enough, but what bothered the doctor was that in the ensuing frenzy following the fire, many of the patients escaped and fled. For most of them, a life of freedom meant little more than wandering until they died of starvation, or were beaten to death by ignorant drunks or cruel teenagers.

But there were also other problems.

When the doctor got to this part of his story he shifted uncomfortably in his chair.

"Come with me, please," he said.

Dinner was over and the doctor now led Clint to a booklined den, where he poured brandy for both of them. They sat in comfortable, leather chairs.

"Have you read any of the local newspapers?"

"No, I haven't been to town at all, yet."

"Well, within the past two months there have been two murders—stabbings of a rather bizarre sort. There was another last night."

"Do you believe this has something to do with the fire and the escaped patients?"

The doctor shifted uncomfortably in his seat and stared into the crackling flames in the fireplace. The look on his face was a troubled one.

"It could," he admitted. "I'm sorry to say that it very well could."

"Did you have violent patients here?"

"A few, yes."

"Men?"

"And women. For the most part I had their violent tendencies under control."

"Through hypnosis?"

"Yes, partly, but I also believe that they were truly violent people—not by their normal nature. I think I was able to convince them of that, as well."

"But now that they are out?"

The doctor sighed heavily.

"I don't know. They might revert," the doctor said, shaking his head. "I just don't know how they'll react being away from me and my treatments."

"Didn't one or two of the murders occur before the fire, before your patients escaped?"

"One did, yes."

"Then how can you be blamed?"

"Ask the townspeople that."

Clint understood. Just having met those two elderly women on the road, he could understand the mentality of the townspeople.

He decided to approach his own problem.

"Doctor, I'm looking for a woman who was or is still a patient of yours."

Clint told Vernon his story of the fire, and how his life was saved by the hunchback, Whitfield, and then told him of Whitfield's request that he find his daughter. Through some of the things in Whitfield's warbag he had been able to put together a rather sketchy description of the girl, but nowhere had he been able to find a name.

"My God!" the doctor said.

"What's wrong?"

"Three of the more violent patients I had here were women. They were all rather attractive, all about the same age, and all the product of orphanages. They all fit your description of this man's daughter."

There wasn't much of a description, except what Clint had been able to piece together himself—certainly, he was able to guess the woman's age, but not much more. He admitted as much to the doctor.

"They all had the same background?"

"That is not as uncommon as it sounds. If they were troubled children, they all could have very well ended up in orphanages."

"And these three women escaped?"

"Yes."

"Do you believe that one of these women could be involved in the murders in Chalmers?"

"It is . . . possible."

"Even before the fire?"

"I had . . . a program by which patients were released on their own responsibility for certain periods of time. And of course, patients could have gotten out at night, and back by morning, without being detected. This is not a prison."

"And attractive women have their ways of getting around . . . rules."

"Yes," the doctor said, nodding.

"You have guards?"

"Yes."

"All men?"

"Yes."

"Have you any idea where I can find these women?"

"I'm afraid so."

"Where?"

"In Chalmers. They are all staying there."

"Wait a minute," Clint said, "let me understand this. They've all escaped, you know where they are, but you haven't brought them back?"

"Perhaps escape is too harsh a word, Mr. Adams. You see, this is a private institute, not a government-funded one. Many of my patients are here of their own accord."

"And these three women?"

"They all came to me on their own, but they all took advantage of the fire to leave without telling me."

"Had they ever discussed leaving this place with you in the past?"

"Yes?"

"And?"

"Luckily, I had always been able to talk them out of it—until now."

"So they took the first chance they had to leave without talking to you—the fire."

"It would seem so."

"How would these women appear . . . to other people, I mean?"

"Oh, they would appear to be perfectly normal. None of them are raving lunatics, if that's what you mean. All appear to be normal, well-adjusted young women—until . . ."

"Until what?"

"Until something sets them off."

"Have you talked with them since they left?"

"Oh, yes. They have refused to come back. They say they are happy in Chalmers. They even have jobs."

"When was the fire?"

"Over a month ago. There was one murder before, and two since, counting last night."

"And they've had time to establish themselves in the town with jobs."

"Yes."

"Have you discussed these women with the local law?"

"The law," Vernon said in disgust. "Where was the law when I was being burned out? Probably right there with a white robe on. No, I have not spoken with the law. I hope to bring the women back here myself, eventually."

"Would you be willing to give me their names?"

Vernon frowned and ran his right hand along his jaw.

"I will give you their names on one condition."

"What's that?"

"I know your name, and your reputation, Mr. Adams. I recognized you almost immediately."

Clint was impressed. Usually he was able to tell when someone recognized him.

"You could find out which one of these women is the killer."

"If it is one of them."

"Oh, I'm afraid it is."

"And what would you want me to do?"

"Turn them back over to me."

Clint thought about it.

"You know I'd be obliged to tell the law about the guilty one."

"But that's what I plan to do, Mr. Adams, only not the law here in Chalmers. I want to turn her over to a Federal marshal, and have her committed to a government-funded institution."

"And the other two? You want me to kidnap them and bring them here?"

"Not kidnap," the doctor said carefully. "I want

you to help me bring them back before . . . something happens. It's for their own good."

Clint gave it some thought again.

"I'll tell you what, Doctor. If I believe that, that those women are better off here with you, I'll help you get them back using any means short of abducting them."

"All right," the doctor said, "yes."

"We have a bargain?"

"Yes."

"All right, then," Clint said, "what are their names?"

NINE

At nine o'clock that night Clint stood on a street corner in Chalmers. The first name on his list was Delores Rafferty. She worked as a ticket taker at the local theater, where a small-town repertory company performed Shakespeare. Clint wanted everyone to be inside and seated before he approached her.

He waited . . .

"Hello."

She looked up, a lovely redhead with huge green eyes and a wide mouth that did not seem to have smiled much of late. The lines at the corner of her mouth did nothing to detract from her beauty. The doctor had said that all the women were attractive, but in the case of Delores Rafferty, that had been an understatement. She was apparently in her early thirties, and had the mature kind of beauty that Clint usually preferred in women.

"Yes?"

"I'm too late, aren't I?"

"Not really. The performance is just getting started. There will be a sermon first."

"A sermon? In Shakespeare?"

"Not really. Dr. Baxter believes in combining religion with social events. He always says that there is no reason that religion must be painful or boring."

"And besides, he has a captive audience, doesn't he?"

"Yes, I suppose he has. Would you like a ticket?"

"I don't think so."

"Then I must close up."

He watched as she closed her little ticket stand, and when she turned, it was as if she were surprised that he was still standing there.

"Are you going to go inside to listen to the sermon?" he asked.

"No."

"Aren't you a church-going woman?"

She looked at him and said, "I do believe in God, but I worship in my own way."

"Nothing wrong with that, I suppose."

"Why do I get the impression that you are not a church-going man?"

"I worship in my own way, too. What will you be doing now?"

"I don't know. Why?"

"We could do something together, since neither one of us is interested in the sermon."

"There is always Shakespeare."

He made a face.

"What would we do, then?" she asked.

He shrugged.

"Go for a stroll. It's a lovely night."

"Yes, it is, but you're a stranger."

"Not if I introduce myself," he said. "My name is Clint Adams."

"Delores Rafferty."

"And now we aren't strangers anymore."

"Maybe not, but that still doesn't mean I'll go for a stroll with you."

"When will you decide then?"

"I have to take this cash inside," she said, showing him a cigar box.

"And then?"

"When I come out, I'll decide," she said, "if you're still here."

"Oh, I'll be here, all right," he assured her. "I am really in the mood to go for a stroll."

TEN

He could see it in her eyes.

What she really thought of him.

This time, instead of hitting her with his open hand he hit her with a closed fist, and as soon as his knuckles came in contact with her face he knew he'd cost himself ten dollars. That was what the madam, Jenny, charged you when you bruised one of her girls. ("Hell's bells, man, you bruise 'em and nobody else wants 'em, just the way nobody wants bruised fruit!")

So then he pulled her to him and started to fondle her big firm breasts, because if it was going to cost him an extra ten, R. D. Greaves was going to make sure he got his money's worth.

She had to help him a lot to get him ready again. The liquor was doing him in and she had taken his load twice tonight already, which was pretty damn good for a man forty-five years of age.

"Use your mouth," he told her, pushing her down to her knees, "and make it wet."

Her hot, wet mouth came down on him and he felt her tongue running over him, and started to get hard again. She fondled his balls and suckled him until he was real hard, but by then he didn't want to let her get up again.

"Right there," he moaned, "take it right there."

So she continued to suckle him until his legs started to shake and then he was ejaculating into her mouth, holding her behind her head so she couldn't pull away, and she had to swallow as much of as she could to keep from gagging...

Afterward he lay down on the bed next to her and dozed, knowing that she would wait patiently until he woke up.

Jenny's girls did exactly what they were paid to do, always...

Later, he left the room and went down the hallway to where the special guests were permitted to take hot baths.

He knocked on the door.

"We're busy in here," a female voice said.

"Yes," a male voice said with a hearty laugh, "we're real busy."

R. D. Greaves, a big, burly man in an ill-fitting vested suit, was not a man given to great displays of patience. He stroked his red beard and made his decision quickly. It was just the kind of impulsiveness that had gotten him fired from the Pinkertons.

He lifted a big booted foot, kicked the door open, and went inside.

In the center of the room squatted a large, ornate bathtub with fluted feet and cut little angels carved into the front. Inside sat a tall, skinny man with a boil on one chin. He looked like a middle-aged farm boy who'd come into a small inheritance and had decided to spend every dime of it in a whoopee house.

The man reared up from the tub, covered with soap suds, pushed past the naked woman who was in the tub with him, and went for his gun. The gun was on a chair too far from the tub for the man to reach without getting out. As he put one foot outside the chair slipped and he started to fall. Greaves helped him on his way by producing his single action Colt .45, bringing the butt down on the man's head.

TRIAL BY FIRE

The yokel rolled his eyes and fell back into the tub with the woman, sinking below the surface.

"Better get him out of there before he drowns," Greaves told the woman. He looked her over and found that she was more girl than woman, with impudent little breasts that look like hard little peaches. Greaves, never a man who could get enough of sex, felt himself hardening again.

"I'll be back in ten minutes," he said to the girl. "I'll expect the same treatment this yokel was getting—maybe even a little better. You hear?"

"Yessir."

With that, Greaves left and went back to the room from where he'd come.

"A little lower."

"Yessir."

"You think you're ever gonna smile for me?"

"Yessir."

"I heard you laughing with that yokel. I want to hear you laughing with me."

"Yessir."

"You didn't like the way I treated that rube, did you?"

"Nossir."

"He was an ugly cuss, wasn't he? You should be glad I got rid of him."

"His wife died in the spring of this year. This was the first time he'd been with a woman since her."

"Ain't that just terrible. Maybe he should have mourned her a little longer."

"You got no call to say that."

"I want you to get in here with me."

The girl had been kneeling by the tub, washing Greaves with soap and a cloth.

"In the tub?"

"In the tub."

"I don't think we could both fit—"

He almost hit her, but remembered the ten-dollar fine just in time.

"Just get in, sweetie, before I drag you in."

As she started to climb in he said, "First get me a bottle of whiskey."

She left, and came back with the whiskey. Once she got into the tub with him he made her drink most of it, which finally got her to laughing with him.

Her body was young and taut, and he knew the longer she stayed here the more used up she'd become. In fact, he intended to use her up real good himself, tonight. He was in one of them moods where it took more than one or two women to satisfy him.

He tossed the empty whiskey bottle out of the tub and grabbed the girl's breasts, pinching them hard—hard enough to make her wince.

"Hey, mister—"

"Shut up," he said. He looked down at the water and saw the tip of his cock breaking the surface, red and swollen.

"All right, sweet girl, mount up," he said.

"In the tub?"

"Right here in the tub, darlin'. I'll slide right on in like a greased pole."

She inched forward and he put his hands under her arms to lift her onto him. Just as he'd promised, he pierced her cleanly, and she sat down on him, taking him to the hilt. She began to ride him and he held her close so he could bite her breasts while she brought him to a climax once again.

Before that could happen, however, the already broken door opened again and a man stepped in, holding a gun.

"Get that little bitch out of here!"

TRIAL BY FIRE

The girl screamed, stood up, and slipped trying to get out of the tub, but retained her feet and ran for the door. Greaves watched her hard little butt with regret as it went out the door. That's where he should have let her have it, he thought, right between those hard little—

The man leaned over and put his gun right in front of R. D. Greave's face, interrupting the man's thoughts.

"You besotted sonofabitch!"

He cocked the hammer.

ELEVEN

While Delores was inside trying to make up her mind, Clint was outside looking in the windows of the shops on either side of the theater. He was studying the men's hats in the window of the hatshop when he heard a woman's cry from across the street.

There, in a pool of light thrown from one of the corner gaslights, was a slight woman striking out against a man with her purse.

Clint sensed that this was not a simple domestic squabble, and crossed the street to see if he could be of any assistance.

When he reached them he saw that it might have been the man and not the woman who needed the help. The blunt, stocky man was trying to duck beneath the blows the young woman was throwing his way with her purse and umbrella. Of the woman Clint got a quick sense of one young and pretty, if somewhat prim.

"What's going on here?" he demanded, stepping between them to separate them, and avoiding a slashing blow with the umbrella in the process.

"He frightened me," the woman said indignantly.

Clint looked at the man. He was not well dressed, and was in need of a haircut. He did not look like a late night Romeo given to accosting young women on the street.

"What did you do to her?"

The man shrugged. He appeared confused, but not drunk.

"No English," he said in an accent that Clint could not readily identify.

"Of course," the woman said. "A foreigner."

Clint smiled.

"Seeing as how this country's a little more than a hundred years old, ma'am, seems to me we're all still pretty much foreigners, here."

"Oh, wonderful," she said, "just what I needed, a history lecture."

"Just what was this man doing that frightened you, ma'am?" he asked. The question seemed ludicrous, because the young woman did not seem the type to be frightened by much of anything.

"Are you a policeman? Or a deputy?"

"No, ma'am."

"Then what are you?"

"Just a citizen who responds anytime he hears a woman cry out for help." He glanced at the man and added, "I may have been mistaken, of course."

"What do you mean?"

"Well, it seems this gentleman here is in more need of help than you are."

"He came up behind me too quickly," she said. "He frightened me."

The man had begun to cower some beneath the woman's hard gaze.

"But he didn't do you any harm?"

"Not unless you consider nearly having a heart attack some harm," she said. "I didn't give him a chance to do much of anything else."

"Why don't we just let him go on his way then," Clint suggested.

"You really are a good Samaritan, aren't you?" the woman demanded. "Well, I'm not impressed."

Clint took the frightened man by the elbow and said, "You'd best be getting along home, friend."

TRIAL BY FIRE

The man nodded gratefully and hurried away without a backward glance.

Clint turned back to the woman. Given the murders that had taken place in Chalmers, he supposed he couldn't blame her for the way she had reacted, but then what was she doing out this late at night, unescorted?

"Miss, why don't I escort you home."

"Because I am not going home."

"It's late, you shouldn't be—"

"I'm going to a meeting at the town hall."

"I see. And where is that?"

"You're a stranger, aren't you?" she asked.

"I guess I'm guilty of that, ma'am."

"It's just up this street. I can get there by myself very well, thank you."

"I'm sure you can, ma'am. What kind of town meeting would be taking place on a Sunday night in a town as God-fearing as this one?"

She frowned and asked, "Are you making fun of us?"

"No, ma'am. I'm just naturally curious."

"We are having a town meeting to decide what to do about Dr. Vernon. Do you know who he is?"

"Yes, ma'am."

"Then you know what kind of man he is. There are some feelings in the community that he is responsible for the recent murders in this town. Do you know about them?"

"Yes, I do. Do you mean personally responsible, ma'am?"

"Not personally, but one of those wretches he keeps in his . . . his institute, as he calls it."

"So tonight you'll all decide if you should burn him out a second time?"

Her eyes narrowed.

"You seem *quite* familiar with the goings on here for a stranger."

"I've heard talk, ma'am, that's all. Perhaps I should introduce myself. My name is Clint Adams."

The woman glared at him, breathing hard. Her small but lovely breasts strained at her simple, high-necked dress. Clint was sure he had met her sort before—the daughter of a locally prominent citizen who found herself displeased by nearly everything God had put on earth.

"The community had nothing to do with the burning of the doctor's other institute," she said firmly.

"Just a few renegades then, eh?"

"Precisely."

With that she jabbed her umbrella in Clint's direction, which he stepped back to avoid, and then tucked it beneath her arm and walked past him.

"Wait."

"What is it now?" she asked, irritated.

"You haven't told me your name."

"Why should I?"

"I've given you mine, it's only common courtesy that you give me yours in return."

"I'm sure that must be one of your favorite words."

"What's that?"

" 'Common'."

Clint grinned despite himself. She was really very good at the insult game—so good you almost had to admire her. She was sharp and quick, as well as pretty.

"Well?" he said.

"Well what?"

"Are you going to tell me?"

She frowned at him.

"If you really must know, it's Louise Hanratty."

And with that she turned and sashayed away, adding a little extra sway to her hips, he was sure, for his benefit.

TRIAL BY FIRE

For a moment Clint stood smiling, watching with interest her hips and backside, but then it suddenly occurred to him where he had heard her name before.

She wasn't the daughter of a locally prominent citizen, at all.

She was one of the other women who had walked away from Dr. Vernon's institute!

TWELVE

After he finished drying and dressing himself R. D. Greaves faced the man with the gun and spoke.

"I wouldn't advise that you ever try that again." The menacing tone in his voice was undisguised. He trembled not from fear, but with anger.

The man with the gun had a white walrus mustache and affected the appearance of a banker, well-dressed and well-fed. At the moment, he was so angry his mustache bristled.

"Never threaten me, sir, unless you mean to back it up on the spot."

With that he once again lowered his weapon so that it aligned itself with R. D. Greaves's chest.

Greaves decided to curb his temper—again, not because he feared the man, but because the man was paying him a goodly sum of money to work for him. It had been Alan Pinkerton himself who had taught him the value of a clear mind—and of a dollar.

"Now, exactly what do you think you are doing in this house of ill repute, sir?" Henry K. Deaver demanded.

"I *was* relaxing, until a moment ago."

"Relaxing? By God, man, you weren't hired to relax. You were hired to find this killer before word of his foul deeds thwarts our plan for a new railroad depot."

Henry K. Deaver did not just look like a banker, he was a banker—in fact, he was *the* banker in the town of Chalmers. He and a group of other men were in competition with a similar group in another part of the state for a new railroad depot. With a crazed killer stalking the streets of Chalmers, it was unlikely that the railroad would choose Deaver's group, who were depending on that depot to increase Chalmers's commerce—and its size.

"Now get back out on that street and start looking," Deaver said. "And have some coffee first!"

"I must remind you, Mr. Deaver, that when you hired me we agreed that you would not question my methods."

"If you got results, sir. There was another murder last night, or hadn't you noticed?"

"I noticed, and I'm working on it."

"Here?"

"Mr. Deaver, can you honestly tell me that you don't make your wisest business decisions when your mind and body are at rest?"

Deaver began to bluster, which led Greaves to believe that he had struck a nerve.

"There's a town meeting tonight, isn't there? I'm surprised you are not attending."

Deaver scoffed.

"Persecuting Dr. Vernon some more is not going to help us find the killer. Dr. Vernon's work is perfectly legitimate. If we didn't have a do-nothing, know-nothing sheriff who pandered to the worst instincts of a mob, I wouldn't have had to hire you at my own expense." He looked at his gun as if he had just noticed that he was still holding it, and put it away. Now he shook a fist at the detective.

"I'll brook no more such incidents as this one tonight, do you understand?"

"I understand you perfectly."

"I have paid you in advance, and in gold, and I expect results."

TRIAL BY FIRE

"Which I have promised."

"Well, by gad, you had better deliver."

With that Deaver turned and left. Greaves looked at the tub, where the water was now tepid, and wondered if it was worth getting the young whore back. Maybe he'd just go back to his room and let the older one finish what the younger one had started.

THIRTEEN

In the glow of a kerosene lamp, Delores undressed, revealing high, pert breasts with chewy pink nipples. She was the sort of woman Clint liked—a bit fleshy in the belly and hips and thighs, tender meat to hold onto during the fires of lovemaking. He watched as she finished undressing, and liked the idea that when she was naked she didn't bother posing for him. She knew it wasn't necessary.

Next, she watched him undress, and he was secure enough about his own body that he didn't mind her watching him. He didn't think she'd find anything . . . too wrong.

When they were both naked they moved toward each other, her reaching out and taking hold of his rigid shaft. Even as they embraced for the first time, she parted her legs so that her moist lips could accept the head of his cock inside her. She wriggled around on his tip, ecstatic.

He kissed her and found her mouth as exciting as the rest of her, hot and fresh and clean, her tongue knowingly moving to meet with his own.

They stood that way for a time, she still dancing on the end of his cock, kissing deeply and wetly, and then gently he moved her back to the bed where she laid back and parted her legs even more, ready to accept the length of him.

Clint, however, was not ready for that yet. Instead he withdrew and began to kiss her breasts, doing to those nipples what was meant to be done to them, chewing them hungrily. She moaned and thrashed about on the bed, holding the back of his head, wrapping her fingers in his hair.

With her fingers still there he began to kiss and lick his way down her body until his mouth and tongue were teasing her wet, slick lips. He licked her and sucked her until she hovered on the brink of orgasm — and then he took her over the brink. Her thrashing became more violent and he held her down, pinning her thighs with his elbows while he lashed at her swollen clit with his tongue.

Before her orgasm could subside, he slid up and entered her, driving his shaft deeply inside her, starting to grind deeper and deeper while she grasped his buttocks, moaning and crying out for more, grinding her pelvis against his, finding and matching his rhythm.

They moved together that way for what seemed like the longest time, her insides pulling on him, sucking at him until finally he was unable to contain himself, and began to fill her with long, powerful spurts . . .

The last thing he had expected was that their stroll would lead them to his hotel room at the Chalmers House. She had seemed intent on simply walking with him a short way and then finding some way to say good night. Sometime during their stroll, however, her attitude seemed to change, and when she had invited herself up to his room, he had accepted readily.

She seemed so normal, and she *was* incredibly lovely. On the other hand, he reasoned, if he was going to find out about her the best way was to get her confidence, and what better way to do that, then . . .

If everything Dr. Vernon had said about her was true, then she was also a very accomplished liar.

"So, until three months ago you lived in New Hampshire?" he asked.

"Ummm."

Three months ago, according to Dr. Vernon, she had still resided in his institute.

"So why did you come to Chalmers?"

"I had decided to come to California, but didn't have a particular place in mind."

"Not San Francisco?"

"When you decide to come to California you already know that you will eventually end up in San Francisco." She continued her story. "Chalmers was the first town I came to that I really liked. I thought I would stay a while and try my hand at some landscape painting."

"You like painting?"

"Very much."

They lay amidst the rumpled sheets of his bed, warm and sweet with the odors of their lovemaking. The kerosene lamp cast a warm glow over the room.

"That's why I took the job at the theater."

"Why?"

"Oh, the people who go there are the cultured people of Chalmers. Or they like to think they are." She smiled. "You know how it is in towns that are growing."

"No, how is it?"

"There is always this little group that fancies themselves the high-class faction, the theatergoers, the well-to-do if not downright wealthy." She paused, then added—as if the words were dirty—"The snobs."

He noticed a change in her voice—not much, but enough to tell him something.

"You don't seem to like these people."

"Oh . . . I wouldn't say that."

He reached for her, but she slipped away and stood up, began to dress.

"What is it?"

"Nothing."

She pulled her dress up, covering her lovely breasts from his view.

"Something is wrong," he said. "What is it?"

"It's just that . . ."

"What?"

"My mother—"

She stopped short and shook her head, as if to dispel some unpleasant thought. The wind screeched outside, branches scratched at the window. The kerosene flame seemed to flutter, threatening to blow out. Her face was in the shadows, away from him now. He stood up and began to dress also.

"What about your mother?"

She sat down on a chair, pulling on her high-buttoned shoes.

"You wouldn't be interested."

"Sure I would."

"Well she—" She paused, seeming to want to choose her words very carefully.

"She was a maid for some very rich people. I used to go to work with her sometimes, to help out. I saw how they treated her, heard some of the things they said to her, called her. The men . . . they thought they could do anything . . . because she was a servant . . . Sometimes I wish I hadn't become interested in art."

"Why is that?"

"The only way an artist can survive is by the grants given them by moneyed people."

The very people, he thought, who mistreated her mother were the ones she had to depend on to support her work—if indeed she was an artist.

TRIAL BY FIRE

Clint felt that her story was probably very true, except for some change in the sequence. Her mother, her art, all that seemed true, but she had obviously come west much earlier than she had said, and sometime during the trip something had caused her to have a breakdown, to go to Dr. Vernon for help—help she obviously felt she no longer needed.

He wondered if her dislike for society people bordered on hatred—a murderous hatred. He would have to remind himself to find out what kind of people the murder victims had been, if they had all been considered to be "society."

He stood up as she was putting on her shawl.

"Why don't I walk you home?"

She looked at him almost sadly. She seemed on the verge of tears, but he sensed a strength in her that would not let her give in at that moment.

"No, I think it would be better if I walked alone."

"But the murders—"

She smiled.

"The killer doesn't frighten me."

"He doesn't?"

"No." She went to him and put her hands on his chest. "I believe he understands the dark side of the human mind. He would sense that I understand it, too."

"Delores—"

"It was lovely, Clint, and I would like to see you again if you stay in town."

"I will be staying for a short time."

"Good. Then we will see each other again."

FOURTEEN

The town hall was a two-story building that sat diagonally across from the hotel.

Clint crossed the street, went up the three broad steps leading to the front door, and went inside, hoping that the meeting would still be in progress.

He wished he had thought of attending the meeting earlier, when Louise Hanratty had first mentioned it to him. Maybe he'd still be able to catch part of it and find out what frame of mind the town fanatics were in.

The place smelled of floor cleanser and kerosene lamps. He followed the light down a hollow-sounding corridor until he came to a double door behind which he could hear the stirrings of an angry mob.

He stepped quietly inside, to listen.

R. D. Greaves stood in the shadows across from the town hall, still not quite believing what he had just seen.

After Deaver had left him, he had gone back to his room, awakened the older whore, and allowed her to finish what the other girl had started, and then paid her and left. He had taken up his present position, waiting to see when the town meeting would break up, when he saw the man leave the hotel just moments after the woman.

He had recognized the woman as the ticket taker from the theater — what a sweet body that one had! —

but when the man left, the recognition was like a physical blow.

Clint Adams, better known as the Gunsmith!

What the hell was he doing here?

Was it sheer coincidence?

Of course, he knew that the Gunsmith was a gunman, not a detective, but he had also heard stories about the Gunsmith solving crimes—murders, even—in Denver, and some other places. He knew that Alan Pinkerton had no liking for the Gunsmith, but that the old man did have a healthy respect for the man. In fact, Greaves knew that the old man felt that very same way about him.

That did not, however, necessarily make he and Adams two of a kind, and he had no intention of letting the Gunsmith catch the Chalmers murderer before he did.

Then something else occurred to him.

He had been in Chalmers for two weeks now, and had not even stumbled over a clue. If Adams was looking into the case, however, maybe coming into it with a fresh point of view—and immediately following another murder—would give the man a good chance of solving it.

All Greaves had to do was follow the man around, let *him* solve it, and then take the credit.

Greaves needed this case to establish his reputation, and his newly formed one-man business.

He needed the credit for this, even if it meant crossing swords with the Gunsmith.

Of course, the possibility did exist that the Gunsmith's appearance had nothing to do with the murders, but Greaves did not like running across a man of Clint Adams's reputation by accident.

Little by little, he actually became glad the man was here, and hoped that it was because of the murders. Coming out on top of the Gunsmith would enhance his own rep even more—especially if the Gunsmith turned up dead, a victim himself of the Chalmers murderer.

FIFTEEN

There were at least fifty peple in the town hall. Clint noticed immediately that what they had in common was not the finery of their attire, nor the eloquence of their tongues, nor their self-control—of which they seemed to have very little—but in what they had in their eyes.

Overzealous eyes.

Crazed eyes.

The eyes of every lynch mob Clint Adams had ever seen.

The meeting hall was laid out much like a church, with pewlike seats stretched from one varnished pine wall to the other, with a narrow aisle down the center. Instead of a deacon's box on front there was a long table where three men now sat, a state flag on their right, and an American flag on their left.

A man in a brown gabardine suit with small, mean eyes and a fancy Stetson on the table in front of him had a shiny sheriff's badge on his shirt.

A man in a blue suit looked as if he were on a diet that consisted of flapjacks and heaps of butter. He sat, bulbous as a toadstool, and harrumphed and got red-faced and shook his wattles every time the sheriff said something.

The third man wore the high, white collar of a preacher, and Clint assumed that he was fresh from his sermon at the theater.

"I say he's got some kind of pact with Lucifer!"

cried one of the people from the pews.

"That is not for us to say," the preacher scolded.

"I don't know about that, Fenrus," the sheriff said to the man, "but I do know one thing. One of his crazies got loose and is killing people here in Chalmers, and I aim to find him."

"You ain't done such a great job so far, Hopkins!" another man shouted.

"You want the job, Angus?" the sheriff shouted back.

The man subsided.

"Now, Sheriff, nobody here wants your job," the fat man said.

"I ain't so sure about that, Mayor."

"I'm behind Sheriff Hopkins here one hundred percent," the mayor said, shaking his wattles again.

"That's because they're in bed together, takin' this town for a bundle," a man in the last aisle said to his neighbor in a low voice.

"Burn the doctor out!" someone shouted.

"And this time make it so's he can't rebuild someplace else again!" another voice—a woman's—added.

"Settle down!" Hopkins shouted.

The sheriff appeared to be in his early fifties, a clean-shaven man with slicked-down hair who seemed to enjoy being up in front of all those people. The mayor—about the same age—seemed ill at ease for a politician in front of a group of his constituents. Clint wondered how far the two elected officials were from another election.

"All I've heard you people talk about for forty minutes now is burning Dr. Vernon out. Now you know I can't go along with something like that."

Which didn't mean that the sheriff was saying that it was wrong.

Smiles broke out all around and Clint recognized

TRIAL BY FIRE 65

the pretty woman he had seen in the street, sitting in a pew toward the back.

"Is that to say that you're going to try and stop us?" someone called out.

"I ain't telling you that, Ethan," the sheriff said, with the tiniest of smiles.

"And you ain't tellin' us it's the wrong thing to do, either, Sheriff," the man called Ethan said. That brought peals of laughter from most of the people in the room.

Up at the table the sheriff seemed unaffected by this, while the mayor and the preacher both frowned — probably for different reasons.

"Hold on, hold on, all of you," the preacher shouted, raising his hands.

When the people quieted down, the preacher continued.

"Now, most of you know that Mr. Deaver has hired a detective to look into this."

"He ain't found nothing yet!" someone shouted.

"The banker is looking out for hisself, and not for this town!" someone else called.

"Give the detective a chance to do his job!" the preacher said.

"We had another murder the other night, Preacher. How much longer should we wait?"

"You could wait at least another seventy-two hours," Clint called out from his position in the back.

All eyes in the room turned to him, because no one recognized his voice. He saw the face of the pretty woman reflect recognition, and then she frowned.

"And just who are you, sir?" Sheriff Hopkins asked him.

"A stranger in town, Sheriff, but a man with an interest in seeing the killer brought to justice."

"And just why might you be interested in catching our killer?"

Clint shrugged.

"I'm interested in seeing any killer brought to justice."

"Would you mind telling us your name?"

"Clint Adams."

He saw the recognition on the lawman's face, and heard the murmurs that went through the crowd as many of them recognized his name, also.

He heard someone mutter, "That's the Gunsmith," and then everyone quieted down again.

"What's your interest, Mr. Adams?"

"I told you, I don't like seeing killers go free to kill again."

"And just what would you do with seventy-two hours, if we gave them to you."

"Find your killer."

"I wasn't aware that the Gunsmith was also a detective for hire."

"I'm not a detective, but let's just say I've got a few ideas of my own."

"And are you for hire?" the preacher asked.

"I am not."

"You'd do this for nothing?" the sheriff asked.

"That's right."

"And what if we refuse?"

"Then you'll be releasing a lynch mob on Dr. Vernon and his people. That's not the job of a lawman, Sheriff. I know you know that."

Hopkins and Clint locked eyes, and the sheriff was the first to look away.

For the first time the mayor spoke up.

"I think it's a good idea."

That drew a sharp look from the sheriff, and the fat man hurried to explain.

"We don't want Chalmers to get a reputation as a lynching town. After all, we are hoping to get the railroad through here."

"I still say Vernon is in league with the devil!" a man shouted.

"Dexter," the preacher said, "you said the same thing about the President of the United States."

That brought laughter from the crowd, which Clint hoped would loosen the crowd up a bit.

"You're siding with Adams?" the sheriff demanded.

The mayor looked nervous, and Clint felt sure that although he had the higher title, he was not necessarily the man in charge.

"I'm just saying that lynching ain't good for a town's reputation. Mr. Deaver has his detective working, and we can have Mr. Adams, here. Between them they're bound to come up with something."

There were murmurs from the crowd, many of them from people who were nodding.

"Well, Mr. Adams," Sheriff Hopkins said, "it looks like you've got your seventy-two hours." The man's sour look made it plain that he wasn't in agreement.

"Thank you."

"But if Adams fails," the sheriff shouted, "it's back to the people for a decision about what to do."

To that the mob reacted loudly, cheering.

The people began to file out then, and Clint stepped aside.

The woman he had seen in the street stopped by him briefly and said, "Good luck to you, Mr. Adams."

"Thank you, ma'am."

The last of the people to leave were the mayor—who left without further word—and the preacher, who stopped by Clint.

"I wish you good luck, Mr. Adams, and thank you for your concern."

"I just want to help, Preacher."

The preacher nodded and left.

"Help who?" the sheriff's voice asked from behind.

Clint turned and saw that it was only he and Hopkins left in the room.

"Everyone."

"Everyone—or are you working for Vernon?"

"I am not being paid by anyone, Sheriff."

"That don't mean you ain't working for him."

Hopkins was a tall man who, with his big fancy Stetson on his head and his hand resting on the pearl-handled butt of a big .45, looked slightly ridiculous.

"I've got a feeling you and me are going to have a run-in before you leave town, Adams—and don't think I'm impressed by your reputation."

"All I'm asking for is a chance to help, Sheriff."

"You've got your chance," the man said. "You've got your seventy-two hours, and after that it's up to me again."

The sheriff left and Clint breathed a sigh of relief. It had been a long time since he'd addressed a lynch mob.

He was pleased that he hadn't lost his touch.

SIXTEEN

The next morning Clint had breakfast in the hotel dining room. He ordered eggs, bacon, potatoes, biscuits, and strong coffee. He never expected much from small hotel dining rooms, but this time found himself pleasantly surprised. During his meal he asked the waiter where he could find the office of the town newspaper.

"That would be the *Republican,* sir. You walk out of the hotel, turn left, and go four blocks. It is also our town library."

Clint thanked the man, paid for his meal, and left.

Upon returning to his room the night before, Clint found that his sheets still held the scent of Delores Rafferty, which initially made it difficult to get to sleep.

He thought about the other woman he'd met, Louise Hanratty. He had only seen her on the street and at the meeting hall, not in her job. Vernon had told him that she worked as a seamstress, so meeting her by accident had saved him the embarrassment of trying to think up a reason to go and see her where she worked, at the dressmaker's.

Lying awake in bed he had also thought about the seventy-two hours he'd requested. The number had simply popped into his head, but he knew he had to do something to keep the mob from burning Dr. Vernon out again. At least he had given the doctor three days grace, and maybe he could find out something during those three days.

He'd finally fallen asleep after deciding that in the morning he would read through some of Chalmers's old newspapers, and seek out the detective who had been hired by the banker, Deaver.

Leaving the hotel now, after a somewhat surprisingly satisfying breakfast, he made his way down the three blocks until he came to the office of the *Chalmers Republican*.

He had another reason for wanting to go to the newspaper office, and she was standing just inside the door behind a counter.

Amy Todd was the third woman Vernon had told him about, and again his comment on the attractiveness of the three was understated. She was striking rather than beautiful—tall and slender with a dark complexion and breasts that seemed slightly too large for her willowy frame. Raven hair reached to the middle of her back, with a single streak of silver shining down the center of it. Obviously, the streak was quite real, but it had a somewhat theatrical effect. She wore a blue gingham dress that seemed a bit demure for her imposing presence.

The front of the office had been arranged as a sort of reading room, with tables and chairs, and a small sofa for more comfort. Arranged in neat stacks inside wide bookshelves were books and newspapers. The room smelled pleasantly of paper, but from the back—where he could hear the press running even now—he also smelled fresh ink.

"May I help you?" Amy Todd asked. Her smile revealed very white teeth, which only added to her luster. Her age was somewhere between that of the other two women—possibly twenty-five, or so.

"Yes, I'd like to browse through some of your recent newspapers."

"Certainly, sir. It would be our pleasure to have you do that. We have a very good selection."

TRIAL BY FIRE

"I was speaking of the town newspaper, the *Chalmers Republican*."

"Of course, I can help you with that," she said pleasantly. "You can look through this shelf over here, on your right. These are all of our papers spanning the past three months."

Her smile seemed genuine, her delight at being able to serve him real. At that moment, however, the door opened and another man stepped in. He was almost disappointed to see her display that same attitude and smile for him, even though he was small and elderly.

He sighed and went to the shelf to check for the facts he needed.

Half an hour later he had learned some facts about the recent murders, all of the information taken from the *Chalmers Republican*.

One thing he had been curious about turned out to be true. The three victims had all been locally prominent citizens, members of Chalmers society.

Each victim had been male, at least forty years of age. They had all been out walking alone at night. Curiously, the papers did not state exactly where the bodies had been discovered.

Two eyewitnesses had reported seeing someone in the vicinity of the killings, but their testimony was too conflicting to be of any help.

One reported seeing a young man fleeing from the scene.

The second reported seeing an old man with whiskers fleeing.

Again, the "scene" spoken of in the newspaper was not identified.

The murder weapon, though it appeared to be the same in each case, could not be identified with any certainty.

The local coroner—who was the town doctor—

leaned toward it being a dagger of some sort.

Sheriff Hopkins, at least as he was quoted in the *Republican,* said he suspected it was a type of sword. Clint wondered what the sheriff's experience was with swords.

The mayor, when asked what he thought, said he had no opinion at all. (Clint could see the man's face reddening, his wattles wattling.)

The *Republican*'s letter column was amusing, if somewhat terrifying on the subject of the murders.

The letters all sounded like a lynch mob being formed in print.

The name mentioned most often was, of course, Dr. Vernon. The majority of the letter writers had no reservations about signing their names to missives that called variously for his a) hanging, b) shooting, c) burning.

A few got very religious and quoted the Bible to prove that Vernon was indeed the devil.

One even went so far as to say that one evening, when he'd been out looking for his lost collie, he'd seen Dr. Vernon standing on the crest of a hill, perfectly silhouetted in a round golden moon. And there before his eyes Dr. Vernon had transformed himself into a wolf . . .

"Is something funny?"

Clint looked up to find himself the object of Amy Todd's warm brown eyes.

"Pardon me?"

"I wondered if something was funny."

Clint shrugged.

"Why do you ask?"

"You were laughing."

"Out loud?"

She smiled.

"Yes."

Clint looked over at the SILENCE sign that was

TRIAL BY FIRE

hanging over the door and said, "I'm sorry. I didn't mean to break your rules."

"It's all right," she assured him. "I like to hear men laugh—when it has a nice sound, like yours."

"Thank you."

"Just between you and me, you're not the only one who finds the *Republican* funny."

"Is it the only newspaper in town?"

"Yes, and it's very vocal in its political views."

"Sounds like someone should start another one."

"Well, it won't be me. Did you find what you were looking for?"

"Yes," he said. He closed the newspaper he had been reading and slid it back onto the shelf.

They talked for a few more minutes before a woman in a pink bonnet entered.

"I left something on my desk for you," she whispered to him quickly.

"What?"

"My address. I thought you might like to come to dinner tonight."

Clint smiled.

"That's very nice of you. Thank you, I'd like that very much."

She went to take care of the woman in the bonnet and Clint left, thinking that making contact with the three women had been very easy indeed.

SEVENTEEN

"Then just how goddamned much *do* you want?"

"Maybe I haven't decided yet."

R. D. Greaves leaned closer. He had to speak low. The lobby was more crowded than a funeral parlor on the day a banker died. Men bearing fancy gold watch chains across their guts and turd-brown cigars in their mouths floated through the blue-smoke haze of the lobby to the barber shop.

He had offered the desk clerk what he thought was a standard bribe for a look inside Clint Adams's room, but the man—perhaps influenced by the number of wealthy individuals in the hotel lobby at the moment—was holding out for more.

"Why you so interested in this one room, anyway?" the clerk asked.

He wasn't much taller than seven feet and he had an Adam's apple bigger than a baseball—or at least, it seemed that way. He had so much grease on his hair that the glare was blinding Greaves, and the smell was making him sick.

"Afraid I can't tell you that."

"Why not?"

R. D. Greaves knew how to slur his words so that people *thought* they heard you say what you wanted them to think you said. It was a talent that he had refined over the years, and he put it to good use now.

Greaves said, "Mergetmentz biddznes."

He knew that he had said it in such a way that the

clerk's imagination would convince him that he had heard, "Government business."

"Shit's sake," said the clerk, jerking up straight, "why the hell didn't you say it was government business in the first place?"

R. D. Greaves said, "I didn't say any such thing, friend, you did."

"Hell's bells," the clerk complained, handing Greaves the key and accepting the previously offered sum of money, "you still shoulda told me in the first place."

EIGHTEEN

For lunch Clint went to a café that obviously catered to the more moneyed people in town. They served beer with two-inch heads, had plenty of free eats (cheese, pink ham, medium-well roast beef), and enough paintings of naked women to piss off an entire chorus of self-righteous, little old ladies. There was even a player piano that seemed to play every tune Clint had ever even mildly disliked.

The talk ran to what you'd expect when men in cravats and spats got together and tried to impress each other with their brain power—the change from gold to silver standards, the impact of electricity, the dubious merits of Benjamin Harrison as President, and how Indians, Italians, Catholics, Socialists, certain types of Methodists, and women who sassed their husbands should, at the very least, be shot, if not first disemboweled and then burned.

It was the standard friendly crowd you met in places where liquor encouraged men to be at their worst.

"What do you think of Harrison?" a man at the bar asked Clint. The man had asked the question before looking at the clothes Clint wore, which were in no way in the same class as what appeared to be the dress of the day.

"Harrison? Frankie Harrison? You talking about my cousin?"

The man gave Clint a pitying look and turned away without further word.

Clint had hoped to pick up some gossip about the killings here but this seemed to be more of a businessman's establishment, and it was business that seemed the number-one topic.

He had ordered his lunch and was starting on his second big-headed beer when he glimpsed a sallow-faced man who looked as if he wanted to be a weasel when he grew up. The man sauntered inside the batwing doors and tried his best to appear tough. Clint noticed the deputy badge on his shirt.

"There's that sissy-assed deputy," he heard a man say. He turned his head and saw a mutton-chopped face looking at the deputy from the next table. He was seated with another man who was white-haired and had a well-cared-for walrus mustache.

Smirks and whispers raced across the room now that someone had started it, and all eyes focused on the luckless-looking deputy, who was even more out of place there than Clint.

"Sissy bastard," Clint heard again, but he noticed how no one was saying it out loud.

The deputy wore a shabby brown suit that even managed to make his shiny deputy badge look dull. He went up to the bar, pulled out a gold coin, tossed it up into the air, then brought it down flat on the bar, slapping the bar hard and shoving the coin at the bartender.

"Eugene," the bartender said sharply, "you know you don't belong—"

"Bourbon."

"Bourbon, my ass," the bartender said. "You know how you get with bourbon, Eugene. Now you just have a goddamned beer or I'll be tellin' your pa."

The businessmen in the place roared. This was exactly the kind of entertainment they liked.

Clint stood up, walked over to the bar, and said to

TRIAL BY FIRE

the bartender, "Give the man a bourbon on me."

The bartender said, "Mister, you don't know what you're doing."

"I figure if a man's a deputy, he ought to be able to have a shot of bourbon when he wants it."

"Only reason he's a deputy is because his uncle's the sheriff and because his pa pisses and moans every time the sheriff up and fires his ass for stone-cold incompetence."

Up close Clint could see that the scruffy, forlorn-looking deputy was younger than he had thought, probably in his early twenties. He smelled a bit, as if bathing was something he did only when Santa Claus was warming up his reindeer, and he wore a ridiculous-looking holster and gun that seemed to be pounds too heavy for him. He had to keep hitching it up so it didn't fall down around his ankles. The worst part of it all was his mustache—if it could be called that. If you put a gun to this kid's head for thirty-seven months he couldn't have grown more than the peach fuzz he had right now.

But Clint was hoping that, given enough bourbon, the kid would be useful to him, so he said aloud, "You folks should have more respect for your lawmen than this."

The line got the laughter he expected it to get, and he then invited the young deputy to have lunch with him.

NINETEEN

The room smelled of sweet, red oily furniture polish that Greaves thought he remembered from his childhood in St. Louis. In addition to a bed and a chipped bureau with a white porcelain washbasin and pitcher on it, there were several mural-style paintings depicting impossibly beautiful sunsets and heroic farm people.

The first thing R. D. Greaves did was take out his gun and hold it ready.

As a Pinkerton, he had learned that there was at least a fifty percent chance that the guy whose room you were in would come ambling in on you.

Greaves got down on his hands and knees and pulled up the side of the blanket to peer into the shadows under the bed. All of the dust motes he'd disturbed sticking his hand underneath made him sneeze.

He put his hand even deeper into the darkness and that's when it happened.

When the red-eyed rat sprang from one corner of the shadows it grasped Greaves's hand so firmly in its teeth that all Greaves could think to do was scream.

Loud.

Greaves pulled his hand out from under the bed and started to shake it, but the rat held on, blood coloring its gray whiskers, mucus of some sort glazing its red eyes. The damned thing was big enough to swallow a cat whole and still have some room left over for six or seven goldfish.

Greaves hopped around for a while, still trying to

shake the ugly creature loose, but he finally dropped to his knees on the floor, almost crying from the pain. He took his gun and began to beat the rat with the butt, slamming it as hard as he could against the sonofabitch's head.

Once.

Twice.

Three times.

When the rat refused to let go, Greaves began banging the bloody thing on the floor, over and over again. until he was convinced that the thing was dead—and still it hadn't released its hold on him.

Greaves was only dimly aware of the door opening behind him, someone having been attracted by the commotion. Finally, he looked up and saw an old gent holding a mop, staring at him. The man pulled a pint of bourbon out of his back pocket, took a swig, and then replaced it. He wore red suspenders over his swollen belly and ran a finger underneath his runny nose, sniffling loudly.

"Help yuh?" the old man finally asked.

"Get this fucking rodent off of me!"

The man squinted at the dead rat and then said, "Only one way to deal with this peckerwood."

And with that the old gent backed up a step, then came forward, launching a kick that sent the rodent damn near into the next county—through the window with a loud crash!

"Mean little bastard, wasn't he?" the old man asked. "Works every time, though."

R. D. Greaves couldn't answer. He was staring down at his bleeding, savaged hand and wondered how this could have happened to a man Alan Pinkerton himself had called, "unsavory, but in every other way professional." (Greaves himself had not been offended by the word "unsavory.")

"You want some more help, young fella?" the old

TRIAL BY FIRE

man asked. He was old enough to refer to the forty-five-year-old detective as a "young" man.

Greaves raised his gun and said, "I don't mean to be ungrateful, old-timer, but if you aren't out of this room in ten seconds, I'm going to blow your constipated hide full of holes. You understand me?"

The old man gave him an unconcerned look and said, "T'aint your room, anyway."

He walked to the door, then turned and said, "I'd get the doc to look at that hand before it falls off."

Gritting his teeth, Greaves rose to his feet. He holstered his gun and then pulled a handkerchief from his pocket and wrapped it around his wounded hand. He knew he'd have to see a doctor so his hand wouldn't get infected, but he was in Adams's room now, and he didn't want to waste the chance. Besides, after the incident with the rat, Adams was sure to hear that someone was in his room.

This would be Greaves's only chance.

Rat bite or no, he was going to find something that he could use.

TWENTY

"That's a mighty interesting story, Eugene," Clint Adams said.

"You mean about the notes?"

"Right. The notes that you aren't supposed to be telling me about."

"The only reason I'm not supposed to tell you—or anyone—" the man paused there to down another bourbon "—about them is because they're the onliest things that link the three dead men together."

"Well, then, I could sure see why the sheriff wouldn't want you to tell anybody about them," Clint said, pouring the deputy another drink.

"You ever met him?"

"Who?"

"The sheriff."

"Yup. Once."

"Personally, I don't care for him," Eugene said, making a face, "even if he is my uncle. Fact is, he makes me nervous. Always yellin'."

"Yelling always tends to make a man nervous," Clint agreed.

Eugene glanced at Clint sharply, almost as if he expected Clint to be having a little fun with him.

"People yellin' at you make you nervous?"

"Of course it does. You know somebody it doesn't?"

Eugene thought a moment.

"Now that you mention it, I suppose gettin' yelled

at *would* make anybody nervous." This was obviously a very real revelation to the deputy, who looked as if someone told him that God was a woman.

"That's what I said."

"And that's exactly why I brought up the subject of them notes."

"I don't follow you, Eugene."

"Because I *don't* like gettin' yelled at. And because I *don't* feel like obeyin' somebody who thinks he can get away with yellin' at me all the time. You understand?"

"I not only understand, Eugene, but I agree. Here, have yourself some more bourbon."

It was not the sort of ploy Clint Adams was particularly proud of.

Taking some dumb-shit kid like Eugene and filling him up with bourbon to pick whatever brains he had for information on the murders.

He didn't really have much choice, though.

Thanks to an uneasy truce with the sheriff and with a mob, he had less than two and a half days to turn up the killer of three men.

The notes Eugene had mentioned sounded as if they might offer the first real clue into the identity of the killer, the first break in Clint's unofficial investigation.

If, that is, Eugene could keep on drinking bourbon without passing out.

The young man's sallow complexion was now even grayer, his dead gray eyes even duller, and his motions as uneasy as a puppet whose strings have been cut.

"I keep tellin' him to check out Pierce Hollow, but he won't do it," Eugene said.

Only occasionally did the men from the bar and from surrounding tables look over. They had gone back to their talk of politics and business. One thing

TRIAL BY FIRE

that Clint had noticed, however, was that the man with the white handlebar mustache had left as soon as Clint and Eugene had sat down. He wondered who the man was.

"Pierce Hollow?"

"That's where the notes said they was to—well, I better not say any more."

"Good."

"Good?" Eugene asked, frowning. "You don't want me to say no more?"

"You're too good a lawman to run off at the mouth, Eugene."

"Yep. That's the God's honest truth. I read me this here book that I ordered from back East called 'Law Enforcement Made Easy'. I memorized nearly every goddamned word in that book, and if I had half a chance, I'd be one helluva lawman—better than my uncle, anyway."

Somehow, Clint was surprised that Eugene knew how to read—which probably wasn't fair to the man. He'd obviously ordered that book to better himself, and that made him smarter than anyone thought.

That was hard to believe, too.

"Eugene, it's hard for me to imagine a more professional lawman than you."

"Are you funnin' me? You tryin' to get me to tell you more?"

"I don't *want* you to tell me more, Eugene. I don't want you getting into any serious trouble with your uncle, the sheriff."

"Trouble?"

"Sure," Clint said, leaning forward and pouring the man another drink, "he'd skin you alive if he knew you were talking to me about Pierce Hollow, wouldn't he?"

"He would," Eugene agreed.

"So I don't blame you for being scared—"

"Who's scared?" Eugene demanded.

"You mean you're not scared of the sheriff?"

"Hello, no. If I wanted to tell you about Pierce Hollow, I'd tell you." Clearly, Eugene's newfound courage was coming straight out of a bourbon bottle, and as he downed another dose, Clint poured him still another.

"I sure do admire you for standing up for yourself, Eugene."

"I mean," Eugene said, wiping his mouth on the back of his hand, "if I was to tell you that Pierce Hollow was where the dead men was all supposed to meet her, why that'd be my business."

"It sure would be. Uh, meet who, Eugene?"

"The lady, the Phantom Lady. The one who wrote the notes that each man got the day he was killed, telling him to meet her in Pierce Hollow."

"Oh, that lady."

"Yeah, that one."

"Well, I know better than to waste any more of my time trying to get information out of you, Eugene," Clint said, standing up. "I'd better get going and let you get on with your job."

"Right," Eugene said, making no effort to stand up, "my job."

"Oh, by the way, Eugene?"

"Yeah?"

"Where's Pierce Hollow?"

"South end of town."

"Thanks."

"Got any more bourbon, Mr. Adams?"

Clint, about to walk away, stopped and said, "Well, I could get you another bottle."

"I'd 'preciate it."

"Still, you'd have to give me something in return, Eugene."

TRIAL BY FIRE

"Like what?" Eugene asked, suspiciously.

"Well, those notes you didn't tell me about?"

"Yeah?"

"You, uh, wouldn't happen to remember what they said, would you?"

Eugene grinned and said, "I got something even better than that."

"Oh? What's that?"

"I got every one of them little notes," he said, indicating his pocket, "right here."

Clint turned and yelled, "Bartender!"

TWENTY-ONE

William Ogden was a haberdasher and a sophisticated one, for these parts—at least, he thought so. Once, if not twice, a year he boarded a train and rode east to New York City where he bought many of the latest men's fashions to bring back to Chalmers.

Ogden was also one other thing: a ladies' man. True, he was a good Lutheran, true, he gave of his time and money to the less fortunate, and true, he backed those candidates with progressive visions, and true, he was a married man—but he did have a failing for the ladies, which was no more in evidence than during his trips to New York City. He simply could not say no to an opportunity to bed an available woman.

On occasion—when the urge came on him—he would go to Jenny's for a girl. The local madam, however, would arrange it so that he did not have to go inside like common folk, but rather would send a girl out to meet him so he could slip her into his carriage and ride out somewhere along the river road, where a spread blanket would become a bed.

(Jenny guaranteed that her girls were disease free. Once Ogden had a miserable trip home from New York, wondering if his burning penis might not be permanently infected, or fall off. Luckily, it was a false alarm.)

In the winter, however, when it was too cold for that, Ogden would dip deeply into Chalmers's supply of married ladies, which carried with it more excitement (one could always get shot) and less risk of disease.

Usually he found his "love" partners right in the store, where they came looking for cravats or suits or topcoats for their husbands. It had been Ogden's experience that many wealthy men married women younger than themselves. Also, they were usually so busy trying to stay wealthy that they often neglected their wives.

That's where William Ogden came in.

(Of course, the women he paired with were by no means all young. One of his most memorable experiences had been with a neglected wife of fifty-two, who had physically dragged him into his own back room, disrobed to reveal a startlingly full and firm figure—for a woman her age—and then set about wearing him out, bringing him to three climaxes—each achieved in a different orifice—in the span of fifty minutes! The very next time she came in she made a purchase for her husband and left without so much as a smile.)

He had no trouble attracting women, either, for he was one of those golden, blue-eyed men whom even other men had to grudgingly admit is handsome. He had thick blond curly hair and a physique he kept in good condition by eating sparsely and by chopping his own wood for his fireplace. He wore Edwardian clothes—the best in his shop—but they only seemed to make his presence more masculine and not at all effete.

Ogden had just taken his latest peek at himself in the full-length mirror he'd brought back from New York when he heard the tinkle of the front bell and heard the familiar voice of Henry, the postman, talking to one of the clerks.

(The full-length mirror always brought back the memory of the daughter of a prominent citizen of Chalmers, seventeen if she was a day, who had insisted on taking him in her mouth in front of the mirror.)

The resplendent forty-six-year-old haberdasher walked out to the front of the store, past the racks of suits and the counters of shirts, underwear, and socks and took the mail from the clerk.

Occasionally he received a forlorn letter from a lonely wife, whose heart he had broken, doused generously with some sweet-smelling perfume or other.

Was there any feeling more powerful on this earth than that of breaking a human heart?

The mail was the usual assortment of bills, circulars, and illiterate hard-luck tales from customers as to why they couldn't pay their bills this month.

With one exception.

The envelope was violet and the perfume enchanting. Positively fucking enchanting.

Odgen rushed back to his private office and opened the envelope there.

OUR EYES HAVE TOUCHED. NOW IT IS TIME FOR OUR LIPS AND HEARTS TO DO THE SAME. TONIGHT AT NINE. I WILL BE AT PIERCE HOLLOW.

THE PHANTOM LADY

Ogden had a great love of secrecy and danger and this letter promised inordinate amounts of both.

Imagine.

A rendezvous at Pierce Hollow.

At a time of the year when frost was on the pumpkins.

And from a woman who was as romantic as himself—"Our eyes have touched. Now it is time for our lips and hearts to do the same."

Marvelous.

William Ogden shivered and consulted his watch.

Nine o'clock tonight could not come early enough to suit him.

TWENTY-TWO

The desk clerk said, "You interested in some information?"

Clint had been on his way up to his room when the clerk beckoned to him.

"What sort of information?"

"Oh, sort of like who might have asked to look inside your room."

Clint hated himself for showing such great interest—the clerk was obviously the sort of man who took great pleasure in manipulating people, watching them squirm—but he was too interested to pretend otherwise.

"Well, who was it?"

"Hey, come on," the clerk said, "do you think information like that comes free?"

"Friend, sometimes information like that comes at the business end of a gun."

The clerk backed up a step and raised his hands in front of him.

"I'm a law-abiding citizen, friend."

"Which is another way of saying that you're a chicken-shit."

"I resent that!"

Clint sighed.

"So who'd you let into my room?"

"Who said I let anybody up there?"

"You're the type, if the price was right."

"It wasn't," the man lamented, "but I let him in anyway."

"And?"

"And then the rat got him."

"The rat? What rat?"

"Seems you had a rat in your room and the government man reached under the bed and—"

Clint's ears perked up.

"Who said he was a government man?"

"Well, he did."

"Did he show you any identification?"

"No—"

"You stupid bastard!"

The clerk flushed.

"You ain't got no right to call me that."

In a single, swift motion Clint leaned across the desk, grabbed the clerk's tie, and pulled him toward him. The guy's breath gave the impression that he had snacked recently on sheep shit.

"Now," Clint said, "I want you to tell me exactly what this so-called government man looked like—and take your time, friend, because you're going to get it right on the first try. Understand?"

The clerk allowed as how he understood—perfectly.

Clint spent twenty minutes in his room checking to see if anything was missing. He could smell the cleaner and disinfectant that had been used to clean up after the rat incident.

Apparently, the "government man's" search had been cut short by the appearance of the rat, as there didn't seem to be anything in the room that had been disturbed.

Then again, there was something that was missing . . .

Clint completed his search before sitting down on the bed to look carefully at the three notes Eugene the deputy had handed him. Clint almost felt guilty about

TRIAL BY FIRE

what would happen to the deputy when his uncle found the notes gone.

The notes all said the same thing, that the men should meet the "Phantom Lady" in Pierce Hollow that night. Clint knew that at least one man was *not* killed in Pierce Hollow. The third man had been killed on the street, but that didn't mean that he wasn't on his *way* to Pierce Hollow.

He tucked the notes away in his pocket and stood up. He was satisfied that there was only one thing missing from his room, and he left to find the so-called "government man" who had obviously made off with the item.

The obvious place to start his search was at the town doctor's office.

Maybe that's where he'd find the man who had stolen his list of the three women's names who had spent time at Dr. Vernon's institute.

TWENTY-THREE

Henry K. Deaver sat underneath a moose head and behind his wide mahogany desk and said, "You promised to report to me by noon."

"I am not a child," R. D. Greaves said.

"No, but you've certainly been acting like one."

Deaver stood up and thrust his thumbs into his vest pockets. He walked over to the window and looked down at Chalmers's main street.

"The railroad people are not going to tolerate another incident like the burning of Dr. Vernon's institute, not if Chalmers is going to be seriously considered for this train depot."

He turned his regal white head back to Greaves and pointed a finger out the window.

"Chalmers needs that depot in order to grow, Greaves, to prosper, and I'll be damned if I'm going to let some lynch mob—or some damned murderer—keep us from getting it. I simply won't have it!"

"I've gotten some results," Greaves said.

"What kind of results?"

"I can't say right now," Greaves said. He patted his vest pocket with his unbandaged right hand, felt the reassuring presence of the stolen list there. "But you can depend on this. I am on the right track."

"You'll damned well tell me what I ask! You work for me, remember?"

"You're not going to get anywhere trying to bully me, Mr. Deaver."

The banker glared at the ex-Pinkerton man, then

relented and said, "Perhaps not. What happened to your hand?"

"I was bitten by a rat."

Deaver sighed.

"Very well, keep me in the dark about everything, but get results, man!"

"I intend to."

Deaver sat down and said, "You seem to have some competition."

"I heard."

"Clint Adams was at the businessman's café today, questioning the deputy."

"That fool?"

"Fool or not, he is a deputy, and he probably had some information for Adams."

Just when Greaves thought he'd gotten the jump on Adams—that damned fool deputy.

"Do you know much about this Adams? Isn't he the one they call the Gunsmith?"

"He is."

"What does he know about detective work."

"Nothing at all," Greaves said with certainty. "The man is completely untrained."

"Tell me, Mr. Greaves," Deaver said, "how soon do you project—"

"I should have your killer in custody inside forty-eight hours."

"That would be sooner than the time allotted to Mr. Adams."

"You did the right thing hiring me, Mr. Deaver," Greaves said. "You'll see."

"Forty-eight hours?"

"That's a promise."

"I certainly hope it's a promise you can keep, Mr. Greaves."

TWENTY-FOUR

There was a tiny smudge of purple ink on her finger from writing the note to William Ogden.

The note about the rendezvous tonight.

She thought of the umbrella . . .

How the blade flashed in the light when she cleaned it . . .

How it winked, reflecting moonlight in the dark when she used it . . .

She smiled, thinking about Ogden.

He thought he was God's great gift to women.

How vain he was about his blond hair, about his white smile . . .

How cruel he was to his wife, cheating on her with every available woman . . .

The voice in her head said that he had to be punished for this, and she agreed.

She thought of the umbrella again, her breath beginning to come faster.

How Ogden deserved the fate he would meet tonight, probably more than any of the others . . .

And how pleased she would be to deliver that fate.

In only a few hours . . .

TWENTY-FIVE

Clint had not found R. D. Greaves at the doctor's office, but he had gotten the man's name, and a good enough description from the doctor to start looking for him.

He decided to start with Chalmers's three saloons and then the restaurants.

He asked at all three saloons, and found a bartender in the third one who knew who he was talking about.

"Pinkerton man," the fat bartender said. He had a yellow, waxy mustache. The place itself had enough antlers on the wall to stock a game preserve. Ornate kerosene lanterns hung from hooks throughout the low-ceilinged place and dispensed not only light but a perfumy oil intended to make the place smell better. There were perhaps twenty men in the place, each with his hat on the bar or table in front of him, and most with huge stogies sticking out of their faces.

"He tell you that?"

The bartender tipped up an invisible bottle.

"Ex-Pinky, anyway. Taking a drink every now and again—and again—ain't exactly something that he's against, if you know what I mean."

"Did he happen to tell you what he was doing in town?"

The bartender shrugged.

"No, that part of it he didn't mention, at all, but I happened to be passin' down the street and I saw him goin' into the back door of the First Savings and Trust Bank."

"I guess you lost me on that one. What would that tend to indicate? That he did his banking through back doors?"

"The back door," the bartender said significantly, "leads to the office of Henry K. Deaver."

"Deaver?"

"Henry K. Deaver," the bartender said slowly, "*is* the First Savings and Trust Bank."

"I see."

"There's a sayin' in this town that the only thing Henry Deaver doesn't want to own is the outhouse and he'd want that if he could figure out a way to gold-plate turds."

"You sound as if he isn't one of your favorite people."

"I ain't friends with any banker."

"What would Mr. Deaver want with an ex-Pinkerton man?" Clint asked, although he had his own ideas along that line.

The bartender shrugged again. It seemed a nervous gesture that had no bearing on his answer to any given question.

"For one thing, ol' Henry don't exactly get along with the law in this town."

"Hopkins?"

The bartender nodded.

"And he ain't exactly tight with the mayor, either. He'd love to see both of them out of office. Also, he's worried about the railroad."

"What about the railroad?"

"They'll be coming through here soon, and there's three towns they could put a depot in. Whichever gets it is in for a big boom."

"Tell me about that."

The bartender had a lot of opinions. It was his opinion that the burning of Dr. Vernon's institute was an act the same as a lynching, and that wouldn't impress the railroad people.

"So maybe ol' Henry hired himself a detective to find the killer before another mob gets a burr under their saddles and grabs some more torches."

That was exactly what Clint was thinking. So now he had a pretty good idea who this fella Greaves was working for, although he hadn't found the man himself, yet.

"Where else might I look for this fella?"

"Well, I did send him over to Jenny's one night, and I understand he's been back there a-plenty, since."

"Jenny's? Is that the local cathouse?"

"It is, and she's the momma cat."

Jenny's would be next, then. If he couldn't find him there, he'd have to go and talk to banker Deaver.

"Thanks for the information," Clint said. He paid for the beer he hadn't touched, and then added something extra.

Clint's stop at Jenny's whorehouse was interesting—a dozen girls prissed and preened for him, of which one or two might have been worth a second look—but it did not produce R. D. Greaves for him.

"He was here last night, but we ain't seen him tonight—yet," the washed-out, fortyish madam said. "Of course, that don't mean he won't be here later. Why don't you take one of the girls upstairs for a spell. Maybe he'll show up in the meantime. How about Lily?"

Clint looked at Lily, who was one of the two he thought might have been worth some time—she had a cute, heart-shaped face and plump breasts—but when he compared this creature to Amy Todd, who was waiting dinner for him, she came out a far distant second.

"Maybe I'll check back later," he said. Tipping

his hat he said, "Good night, ladies," and backed out.

This time R. D. Greaves had better luck with his illegal entry.

He waited until long, purplish shadows stretched across the streets, until lanterns lit in the lacy windows of the respectable homes, and then he made his move.

Aided by a set of burglar tools he'd appropriated back in his Pinkerton days, he managed to break into the apartment of the first name on Clint Adams's list and damned if within three minutes he didn't up and find exactly what he was looking for.

Exactly.

He smiled to himself and thought of the bonus Henry Deaver had promised him.

Within a few hours, on this night, he would have his proof, and he would have his killer.

TWENTY-SIX

Clint would have continued his search for R. D. Greaves but for two things: the bank was closed, and he did have Amy Todd waiting for him.

Of course, he could have braced the banker at his home, but he chose to return to his hotel to freshen up and walked along the dark streets to the address that Amy Todd had left for him on the piece of paper.

Amy lived in a small house just this side of where the board sidewalks ended. Across the street stood a respectable two-story house with a buggy set in the roadway, a horse sort of talking to himself in the darkness. The only thing that made the buggy remarkable was the fancy carriage-style lights on one of its arms.

Clint paid the buggy no more attention. He walked to the door of the trim little house with the slanted brick chimney and knocked once.

Behind the door he thought he heard the sounds of more than one person moving about quickly, and he knocked again.

This time the door opened but as it did Clint thought he heard a back door slam.

"Well, hello, stranger," Amy Todd said.

She looked especially becoming with her long, silver-streaked hair combed down the center of her back. She wore a man's faded blue shirt and jeans. The one cute touch was the lacy apron she wore around her waist.

"Come right in."

Clint did so, but as he did he heard the buggy across the street moving away.

The house smelled cleanly of turkey, and of baking.

"Is everything all right?" she asked.

"Fine," Clint said. "I was just taking in the cooking odors. If it tastes as good as it smells, it stands to be one fine dinner."

"It will be," she promised. "Can I pour you a brandy? I still have a little work to do in the kitchen."

"That sounds very good."

"Good. Why don't you sit down and I'll bring it to you?"

"I appreciate it."

He sat and watched her do all the things a woman who was entertaining a man was supposed to do. What most impressed him was how much she seemed to be enjoying it all. She handed him a brandy snifter and waited to see if he approved of the taste before excusing herself and going back to the kitchen.

Clint wondered if he *had* actually heard a back door slam, and if the buggy across the way leaving as he entered had been a coincidence.

While he waited he leafed through some newspapers, then took the opportunity to walk around the room, carrying the brandy with him. At one point he noticed the umbrella leaning against the wall.

It could easily have been mistaken for a man's umbrella, except for the slender furl and the delicate ivory handle.

He remembered seeing it somewhere before—

Where?

"Dinner's ready," she announced. She had entered the room and was wiping her hands on the apron. "I sure hope you're hungry."

"Oh, you don't have to worry about that," he said, enjoying the thrust of her breasts against her shirt.

When they were seated across the table, he sought

in her face some resemblance to Whitfield, the man whose daughter he was in search of, the man whose daughter stood to inherit a fortune in diamonds.

Stolen diamonds.

Something occurred to him over dessert. Dr. Vernon had said that all three women were about the same age, yet Louise Hanratty seemed so young, and Delores so mature. Amy Todd, on the other hand, seemed to be somewhere between the other two women. Young, yet mature.

He'd have to check with Vernon on their exact ages. There had to be some difference.

TWENTY-SEVEN

R. D. Greaves said, "You cut me an extra piece of pie, would you, now?"

The waitress, smiling down at his formidable belly, said, "You sure you got room for it?"

Greaves smiled.

"Oh, I've got room for it, all right, sweetie."

She brought him a big, gooey piece of rhubarb.

"Mmmm," Greaves said.

She laughed.

"You sure take your pleasures in a public way, mister."

She was forty if she was a day, but she did have large, sumptuous breasts.

"Some pleasures are best taken in private, though, don't you think, darlin'?"

She disregarded what was obviously an attempt to embarrass her and nodded out the window he'd been staring out for two hours.

"You must see something out there that I sure don't see."

"How's that?"

"Well, you been starin' out there for nigh onto two hours now, and all I see is the haberdasher's—and that's closed."

Greaves grinned.

"Is that a fact now?"

She squinted at him and said, "You after ol' Billy Ogden?"

"Why would I be?"

"He might have taken a liking to your wife, or something. It's been known to happen with ol' Billy, right there in that shop of his."

She had such a melancholy look on her face that Greaves swore she must have been speaking from experience.

"No, I ain't after Mr. Ogden."

"Then why you keep starin' at his place?"

"Right now, I'd just kind of like to stare at this here piece of pie—unless you got something better in mind, that is?"

She smiled and left him sitting there, watching the dark window of the haberdasher's across the street. Occasionally, he'd taste a bit of his pie. It was real sweet, just the way he liked his pie and his women. Thinking of women made him think of that young girl he had in the tub with him yesterday when Deaver broke in on him. He'd sure like to get that one back.

Then again, this waitress sure seemed a solid sort, heavy in the breasts and hips, with a real chunky backside . . .

For an instant he thought he saw a light way in the back of the haberdasher's, and he pushed his chair back a ways, excited.

From what he had learned going through the woman's room earlier, the haberdasher—William Ogden—was going to be the next victim.

He could have warned the man, of course, but then he might have panicked and scared the woman off. Where would R. D. Greaves's bonus be then?

He already had big dreams of taking that money to Denver and staying at the Willard Hotel where they actually had an indoor swimming pool. You could also find the most delightful prostitutes—clean of teeth and orifices—imaginable.

TRIAL BY FIRE

But when he looked again he saw that there was no evidence of movement or light and he wondered if it hadn't been the trick of some light reflecting off the plate glass window.

He went back to his pie.

And his watching.

TWENTY-EIGHT

Her breasts were full and round and firm, her nipples pink and large.

Following dinner and dessert Amy had asked, "Would you like some more pie? Or some other form of dessert?"

Her meaning did not escape him.

"I would love another form of dessert."

She led him to the bedroom, and put out the lamp. Now moonlight cast a silver bar across her bed and she slipped from her man's shirt and jeans and stood pale white and slender before him—except for those breasts. In the moonlight he could see the outline of her ribs, but her breasts were as full as they could be, and she bore them proudly.

He was out of his own clothes in moments. He crossed to her and instantly pulled her to him. He felt the bounciness of breasts, and the rasp of her pubic hair.

He slid one hand around her and in response she lifted one of her legs so that his penis could play gently against her lips while they were still standing.

They played like this for a time—her lips becoming more and more moist, and he slipping more and more of himself into her—until she finally disengaged herself and slid herself down the length of his body. She began to lick the length of his shaft. She almost consumed his balls and his penis.

She was incredibly skillful.

Just as she worked him to the brink of exploding,

he pushed her gently back onto the bed and started working on her with his own tongue. He went rigid as he worked on her, and then would relax, and then go rigid again, and he just kept on licking her, burrowing his tongue deep, until finally she screamed and reached for him.

He seemed to fill her up entirely as he started stroking her. In the moonlight as he looked down at her that silver streak down the center of her hair seemed to shine. Her hair was so long that she wrapped it around both of them as they slammed into each other. She wrapped her legs around his hips and fought to take him even deeper, until finally they achieved a climax together, the crest of which they rode wrapped up in each other's arms . . .

William Ogden lived above his haberdasher's shop with his wife, Emma—which, of course, made dallying with women *in* the shop even more exciting, knowing that Emma might walk in on them at any moment. Emma was a decent woman and, when they had married more than twenty years ago, she had been a pleasant enough looking woman, but she had put on extra pounds in her waist and hips until now she looked as if she were carrying around something extra inside her clothes, all the time.

Ogden heard the even breathing of his wife and slid out of bed without waking her. He dressed quickly, his heart beginning to beat more rapidly as he went over the contents of the note again in his mind.

His Phantom Lady was waiting, and he didn't want to keep her waiting any longer than he had to.

"You ain't gonna finish your pie?"

"No, I don't have time," Greaves said, pushing back from his table.

"Is something wrong with it?"

"No."

"Is something wrong out there?" she asked, looking out the window.

But Greaves wasn't there to answer her, to tell her that he had just seen the haberdasher leave his place and start walking—somewhere . . .

He'd flung down some money and had already left.

Usually, following lovemaking, there was a peaceful time in the darkness when lovers were left to their own thoughts, most often about the person lying next to them.

What Clint Adams was thinking about, however, was the curious sound of a back door closing, and of the carriage suddenly leaving as he entered Amy Todd's house. He was also thinking of that curiously familiar-looking umbrella . . .

"Wish I had a penny," Amy Todd said.

"Why is that?"

"I'd give it to you and then you'd have to tell me what you were thinking."

"I was thinking of how nice it was."

She sighed.

"Yes, it was." She laughed and said, "Clint, you're the sort of man I've always wanted to know."

"What kind of man is that?"

"Oh—" she started, then paused. "Well, I grew up under rather strange circumstances."

"Really?"

"Yes. My mother was a—a madam. I'm afraid that living in a whorehouse, I got the wrong impression of men. I saw them at their worst, so . . ."

There was no sense of rancor or bitterness in Amy's voice when she talked about men, just a sense of sadness, of disappointment.

"You're different. You cared about—well, about my pleasure as well as your own. I wonder if you know how rare that is in a man."

"A man's got to please his partner, Amy, or she won't want him back."

"Well, Mister Adams," she said, turning over and whispering in his ear, "you're invited back here anytime the desire strikes you."

"You mean . . . like now?" he asked, leaning over and kissing her on the mouth.

"Already?"

"Unless you object—"

She pressed herself up against him and said, "Never, never."

She slid down and took him in her mouth again. It seemed to be what she most enjoyed, having a man in her mouth, being in control. She slid her hands beneath his buttocks and sucked on him noisily, and the sounds she made caused him to become even more excited.

"Amy—" he said hoarsely.

She released his penis, laughing gently. It glistened and pulsed in the moonlight and she gave it one last flick with her tongue before she mounted him.

She rode him then, her big breasts dangling invitingly in his face. He reached for them and pressed them together so he could bite both nipples at the same time. Her breasts were large enough to allow that, but it was obviously something that she had never experienced before. She came immediately as a result of it, and then again as a result of riding him furiously, and then he was filling her with his seed, laughing himself . . .

Later he dressed as she slept, and noticed that her sleep was not peaceful. He felt for a moment like getting back into bed with her and cuddling her, telling her everything was all right, but she obviously had her own personal demons to reckon with.

He wondered if those demons had led her to murder.

TWENTY-NINE

Clint found the livery stable still open even though it was half past eight, and told the Negro in charge that he wanted Duke.

"We gonna close soon, mister. You sure you got to take this ride?"

"Just leave me the key and I'll put him up when I get back."

"I can't leave you the key, mister—"

Clint took out some money and shoved it into the man's hands.

"Is that enough to buy the key for the night?"

The man counted the money and said, smiling broadly, "Mister, this here's enough to buy the whole kit and caboodle."

"That's all right," Clint said. "All I want is the key."

The man gave Clint the key and then went off to spend some of his not-so-hard-earned money.

Clint, saddling Duke, wondered himself if he really needed to take this ride, but there were some things he wanted to talk to Dr. Vernon about, and he didn't want to wait until morning.

Clint talked softly to Duke, asking the big gelding how he was, stroking his massive neck, and then ten minutes after he had entered the livery he was on his way to Dr. Vernon's institute, which was only about fifteen minutes away.

As Clint approached the front entrance of the institute, a man appeared holding a double-barreled shotgun. He looked Clint over and, apparently remembering him from the day before, waved him inside.

A squat woman opened the door to his knock, listened to his request, and then took him down several long corridors to the large den where he found Dr. Vernon.

Vernon was wearing some sort of a smoking jacket, and had been reading a book that he now set aside.

"This must be serious, for you to ride out here at this time of night. Have you found the killer?"

"No, but I have some questions that need asking, and answering."

"What questions?"

Clint took out the letters he'd gotten from Eugene and handed them to Vernon.

"What do you make of these?"

Vernon glanced at them. He was holding a hand-carved pipe and put it in his mouth so he could study all three of the letters.

"Where did you get these?"

"From a drunken deputy named Eugene."

"But how—"

"That doesn't matter. What matters is that all these notes were found on the three dead men. What can you tell me about the handwriting."

"Well," Vernon said, frowning, "it's most definitely the same in each case—"

"Not that. Do you recognize the writing?"

Vernon studied them again.

"No, I can't say that I do."

"Look at them a little closer."

Vernon moved over to a lamp with the letters when there was a knock on the door.

"Yes?"

The stout woman stuck her head in and said, "I'm sorry to disturb you, Doctor, but it's Mitchell. He's

TRIAL BY FIRE

had a dream and needs to be restrained."

"Of course," Vernon said. "I'll be right there." He put the letters on the table and said to Clint, "You'll have to excuse me, I'm afraid."

"Of course," Clint said. "I understand."

As Dr. Vernon went to take care of his patient, R. D. Greaves peered down a long, dark road to where William Ogden was walking. Obviously, wherever he was going he did not need a horse to get there.

The man was rushing, though, taking no chances with being late—even though Greaves knew that the man was at least half an hour early.

William Ogden entered Pierce Hollow and saw the cabin immediately. That had to be where the love tryst was to take place.

Ogden thought briefly of his wife at home in bed, but then became a slave to his lust, to the challenge of a new woman, and hurried toward the cabin, wondering if she were already there, early and as anxious as he was.

While the doctor was gone Clint paced the den.

He was surprised that Vernon did not seem to recognize the handwriting. Or perhaps "disappointed" was a better word. You would have thought that at some time the man would have seen the handwriting of the three women—

Near the fireplace was a wing-backed leather chair that Vernon had obviously been seated in before Clint entered the room. On the right arm of the chair lay a book, facedown, still open to the page Vernon was reading.

Clint glanced down at the title: *Interpretations of Franz Mesmer's Work, and its Effects on the Criminally Insane*.

Mesmer was the man Vernon had told him about. On impulse he picked up the book. He felt that he needed to know more about Mesmer's work, and about the derangement that would cause one of the women he had met to kill.

Was it Delores, the red-haired beauty?

Or the silver-streaked, skillful Amy Todd?

Or was it the doll-like Louise Hanratty who was the murderer?

And which of them was Whitfield's daughter?

Vernon reentered the room then and said, "That wasn't so bad. Would you like some wine?"

"No, I don't think so."

Vernon noticed the book in Clint's hand.

"Are you interested in that?"

"Yes, very much."

"Take it with you then, read it. It might help you."

"Thank you. I was thinking the same thing myself. Can we get back to—"

"The letters, yes," Vernon said. He picked them up again and examined them.

"I wish I could help you with these, but I'm afraid there's nothing about the handwriting that is in any way familiar."

"Well," Clint said, taking the letters back, "it was just a chance . . ."

"What about that wine?"

"All right."

Vernon poured them each a goblet of wine and passed one to Clint.

"Have you met all three women?"

"Yes, I have. I've spent more time with two of them, but I need more time with Louise Hanratty."

"They're all lovely, aren't they?"

"Yes, as a matter of fact, they are quite beautiful. There's something I don't understand, though."

"What's that?"

TRIAL BY FIRE

"Their ages. Delores Rafferty seems older, more mature than the others, and Louise Hanratty seems so young . . ."

"I assure you, Clint, they are all very close in age."

"Do you have their records?"

"Records?"

"Their files? I'd like to see them, check their dates of birth—you do keep files on your patients, don't you?"

"Yes, of course, but—the fire. They were all burned in the fire. My assistant and I are working on reconstructing them, but it will take some time, I'm afraid."

"I see."

Another disappointment. It seemed to be Clint's night for them.

"Well, I'd better be heading back."

"You didn't finish the wine. It will warm you."

"Wine would warm me, but I would have preferred information."

"I'm sorry I can be of no further help. I'll walk you out."

Walking down the corridors Clint thought he could hear the sounds of men and women crying out.

"They get worse at night," Vernon explained. "Many of them have trouble sleeping. The night magnifies their fears."

"How do you sleep?"

"You must inure yourself to it—harden yourself. That's the only way you can help them, really. If I start to feel sorry for them, I would be lost."

At the front door they shook hands, and Clint thought about the last thing the doctor had said.

About being lost.

THIRTY

William Ogden sat in the darkness of the cabin, waiting. His cigar was a glowing nub. He suspected that the scent of his cologne had mostly worn off. And even in his fur-collared winter coat, he was cold.

Whenever he wanted to check his expensive pocket watch, he strode to the window and held it up to the glow of the moon shining through the cobwebbed window.

It was well past nine.

Well past.

For the first time Ogden asked himself the question that should have occurred to him the first time he read the mysterious note.

Was some woman toying with him?

Then the darkness and the cold inspired an even more insidious notion: What if a jealous husband had lured him out here?

Ogden shivered.

He was not a brave man.

Once again he consulted his watch, almost in the way a gypsy consults tea leaves, looking for some kind of truth among the numbers on the watch face.

But there was nothing—

Just the darkness—

The cold—

R. D. Greaves sat behind a large boulder off the side of the road. He was less than one hundred feet from the cabin.

He had known, since this afternoon, the killer's identity. But now he had to prove it. If this meant that Ogden had to die in order to gain such truth, well, R. D. Greaves had never pretended to be a noble man.

At this moment R. D.'s horse chose to rid himself of his dinner. Big brown dripping plops hit the ground, and steam rose from them.

R. D. went back to staring at the cabin. He just wanted to get things over with so he could get back to his room and make out his report. That was one thing he had learned from Alan Pinkerton. Write everything down in what Pinkerton called a "narrative" style so whenever your client had a question, you just consulted your report. You appeared thoroughly professional and the client complained less—at least to your face—about your bill.

While watching for Ogden to leave his haberdashery tonight, Greaves had written much of his report. Now it rested, folded neatly, inside his suit jacket.

The sweet-acrid odor of horse shit wafted up to Greaves's nose again and he turned to see if the animal wasn't stirring it up, somehow.

That was when R. D. Greaves, filled with rhubarb pie and dreams of idle sinning in Denver, was stabbed precisely in the middle of the throat by a blade that both smashed his larynx and ripped a perfect two-inch gash across the right side of his neck.

He wanted to scream but discovered—among all the other horrors filling his mind—that he had lost the simple ability to speak.

Leastways, noise that anyone could hear. In his mind, Greaves was screaming . . .

And then he fell forward and died.

He would have appreciated the irony of where he landed, face first.

• • •

TRIAL BY FIRE

William Ogden thought he heard something outside the cabin. He immediately got up from the wobbly bench on which he sat and went to the window.

Then he made a decision that filled him with a certain amount of pride.

By God, he would go out there and find out what was happening.

For a man not given to great displays of courage — other than having sex with other men's wives — that was a decision to hold your head up high about, to swell your chest over, to share with fellows over whiskeys when men turned to extolling their own virtues.

The cabin door creaked as he opened it.

Before him was a clearing of autumn-brown grass at the edge of which was a road. Beyond that was one of those huge glacial boulders the floodwaters had deposited here thousands of years ago. (William Ogden's favorite school topic had been history.)

In the moonlight, the horse's head was visible, peering out from behind the tall boulder.

Ogden gulped, listened to the night for some clue as to what might be going on. A barn owl hooted. A coyote bayed for food. Distantly, a train rumbled through the western darkness.

Ogden decided to cross the road and see what the horse was doing there.

He was only a few steps from the animal when, from behind him, he thought he heard another sound.

He turned his back completely on the boulder and looked back across the distance he had come.

Up on the little shelf of hillock the cabin sat, dark, waiting . . .

Was that where the noise had come from?

He touched his nose, rubbed it. Cold. He needed to urinate, too.

But he listened as intently as he could for the noise

again. Sound carried so well on nights like this, it sounded almost as if something in the cabin had been bumped.

That was impossible. He'd been in the cabin and he knew nobody was there.

Nobody—

He turned back to the boulder.

Gulping once again, wishing now that he had stayed in bed next to his wife, where it was warm, he eased himself around the boulder, nervously balling his hands into fists.

There, he found the man—

It was one of those odd moments that are both terrible and comic at the same time.

Terrible because he was obviously a dead man, dark blood pooled around his shoulders and outstretched arms.

Comic because when he'd died, he'd fallen straight down, face first, into a fresh pile of horse shit.

But within moments any humor, however absurd, left William Ogden as he stared down at the chubby man in a cheap suit. (Being a haberdasher, Ogden would not forgive even a dead man for poor taste in clothing.)

Suddenly, overwhelming panic seized him and he fled, arms wide, back toward the cabin, his silhouette against the golden circle of the moon that of a scarecrow come to life.

He would have taken the horse and fled, but he wanted to make sure he had left nothing behind in the cabin that would tie him to this time and place.

The cabin's gloomy interior still smelled of mildew and mud.

He reached for the small kerosene lantern to light it, when he heard the floor board creak and realized in that instant that he *had* indeed heard something in the cabin—

"Oh, my God!" he cried, throwing his hands in front of his face. He knew he couldn't escape death, but neither did he want to see it coming.

His killer advanced without hesitation and the blade —long, sharp, and still warm—flashed in the moonlight.

"Please! Please!" he begged, cowering.

But it was no use.

The first thrust hurt—it hurt like hell!

He never felt the second one.

THIRTY-ONE

Clint reined Duke in not far from the large boulder where Greaves had been killed. He'd decided that on the way back to town he'd stop by Pierce Hollow and take a look.

Duke was instantly troubled. Over the years Clint had come to appreciate the big gelding's instinct for trouble. He trusted it almost as much as he trusted his own.

Clint dismounted and started a search of the woods surrounding the road. It only took him a few minutes to find the body.

From the description that had been given, the dead man was the mysterious "government man"—the banker's hired detective. With his toe he rolled the man's face out of the horse shit he was lying in, bent over, and went through his pockets. He found a sheet of long paper, neatly folded lengthwise, that was written in impressively neat longhand. He also found the list of names that had been taken from his hotel room. He put both in his pocket. He found the detective's wallet, and found that the man's name was Richard Devon Greaves, an ex-Pinkerton.

He'd never heard of him.

A study of the ground told him that there was a horse there not long ago. It only confirmed what the fresh horse shit had already told him. He looked up the hill and saw the shack. The "Phantom Lady's" rendezvous, no doubt.

He walked up to the cabin warily, but his own

instincts were working now. Something had happened here some time ago, but right now he felt there was no danger. He went through the door of the shack with his gun still holstered. He could get to it quickly enough if he needed it.

What he found inside the shack were the hacked-up remains of a man, probably the next victim of the killer. The detective had simply been in the right place at the wrong time, and been killed, as well.

For a time he stood outside the cabin, going over in his mind the chain of events that had brought him to the scene of this slaughter. Getting the letter from Whitfield that would entitle one of the women to a fortune in stolen diamonds, meeting Dr. Vernon, investigating the three women who had walked away from his institute.

Which of the three of them was Whitfield's daughter—if it was any of them?

And which of them was a killer—again, if any?

And if one of them was a killer, was it Whitfield's daughter?

Down on the road Duke neighed. Clint became afraid that someone would discover the bodies, and a lynch mob would immediately form. They would undoubtedly go out to the institute to exact their revenge.

As wrong as he knew it was, he decided to move Greaves's body into the cabin. That way, no one would find it by accident, and it would give him some time to work with.

The man was heavy—heavier in death than he must have been in life—and by the time Clint got him into the cabin he was sweating and breathing in hard rasps. He'd thought about burying both bodies, but that would have taken too much time and effort, and would have been indefensible in the eyes of the law. He could always say that he moved the other body into the cabin to keep the wild animals from getting at it.

Sure.

And then he forgot to tell anyone that both bodies were there.

Clint rode back to town, used the key to open the livery, and put Duke up, then went back to his hotel room. He realized how filthy and sweaty he looked—and how he smelled—but it was late and the streets were sparsely traveled. Only the desk clerk was in the lobby, but he didn't give Clint anything more than a disinterested glance.

Upstairs he poured some water into a basin, removed his shirt, washed himself, and then put on the clean shirt and pants. After that he sat down on the bed to read what the detective had written.

He couldn't help but be impressed by the preciseness of the report. He read it through twice, then put it down and shook his head.

He had no idea what kind of a detective R. D. Greaves might have been, but in this instance the man just might have come up with the identity of the killer.

THIRTY-TWO

Henry Deaver's house resembled an antebellum mansion, complete with Grecian columns, all on a somewhat smaller scale than the original.

Clint had walked there from the hotel, deciding to brace the banker in his home at this ungodly hour. He wanted the man off balance.

Clint knocked, and the sound was as loud and obtrusive as a gunshot.

The man who answered wore a comic nightshirt and nightcap. He was a man in his sixties, white-haired with a large, white handlebar mustache. He was the man Clint had seen in the businessman's café.

"Yes? Can I help you?" the man asked.

Clint felt that the man must have recognized him, although there was no outward appearance of that. Still, a man awakened at this hour would not respond so calmly under normal circumstances.

"I'd like to speak to Mr. Deaver."

"That's impossible," the man said. "It is late and the family have all retired."

"I still need to talk to you, Mr. Deaver."

As soon as the banker realized that Clint knew who he was, he became officious. It was probably the way the man dealt with everything.

"What is it you want?"

"I have some news you're going to want to hear."

"At this hour of the night? It's nearly midnight, you know."

"I realize that."

The man compressed his lips in annoyance, then stepped back and said, "Very well, come on, then."

Clint entered, and the man closed and locked the door.

"We can talk in my study."

Clint followed him to another room that was lined with books. The man closed that door behind them, then turned to face Clint.

"What is it, then?"

"I found this tonight, on the body of a man called Greaves."

He handed Deaver the handwritten report. After all, the man was paying for it.

The older man took the paper and stared at it, and then the true meaning of what Clint had said sunk in.

"Greaves is dead?"

"Yes."

"When did this happen?"

"Tonight."

"Where?"

"In a wooded area near Pierce Hollow."

"How did he die?"

"He was stabbed. Surely that mode of death sounds familiar to you?"

"My God. What on earth was he doing out at Pierce Hollow."

"My guess is he followed the next murder victim, and became a victim himself."

"You mean—"

"He wasn't the intended victim, Mr. Deaver. The murderer killed him, and then took care of his or her true victim."

"You mean . . . there's been another killing?"

"I found both bodies."

"Who was the other hand?"

"His identification said he was Henry Ogden."

"The haberdasher?"

"If you say so."

"But what was he doing out there—" the banker started, but then he stopped. "For that snake to be involved, there had to be a woman somewhere."

"I'm sure he was going there to meet a woman for what he thought was a romantic assignation."

"And he was killed for it?"

"Yes."

"A jealous husband, no doubt. I think you're mistaken, Mr. Adams." Clint didn't mention the fact that Deaver had originally pretended not to know who he was. "This murder has to be a coincidence."

"I don't think so."

"Why not?"

"Because all of the victims were on their way to Pierce Hollow, as well. Some of them made it, some of them didn't."

"Why would they be going there?"

"To meet a woman."

"You mean . . . a woman is the killer?"

"It's beginning to look that way."

"That's preposterous. How could a woman commit these monstrous crimes?"

"Maybe if you read that report that you've already paid for, you'd find out."

Deaver looked at the paper in his hand, then back at Clint, then nodded slightly, as if to himself, and began to read.

"We'll have breakfast in the morning and talk about it. All right?"

Clint didn't wait for an answer, he just opened the door and left. In the morning he was planning to have a huge breakfast, on Banker Deaver, of course.

When Clint got back to his hotel he pulled out the

book on mesmerism that the doctor had loaned him and started to read it. He quickly established two things.

Number one, mesmerism—or hypnotism—was something that he would like to see in person.

And two, the book was far too complicated for a layman like himself to understand.

He set the book aside and went to sleep.

THIRTY-THREE

She washed the blade off in the basin and then went in to sit by the window and look at the way the moonlight made shadows that played in the street.

It was so peaceful this time of night—

So peaceful right after a killing—

She thought of the killings over the past three months, and how the voice in her head made her do it.

The voice was talking even now . . . and then, abruptly, it stopped.

She tried not to think about the voice after it stopped, because she knew it would come again, echoing inside her head, making it hurt.

The voice would urge her . . .

Command her . . .

She took the brandy decanter she had saved up to buy and poured herself a healthy glass. Dr. Vernon used to give her brandy from a decanter like this one.

Holding the glass, she let her head rest against the back of the chair.

Allowed her eyes to close.

She tried to forget everything that happened at Pierce Hollow tonight.

Tried to fill her mind with a lullaby she remembered her mother singing to her when she was very little, before she had been put in that orphanage.

She allowed the peaceful melody to fill her mind and forgot how she had slashed and cut and hacked—

Almost as if she'd had no choice . . .

As if the blade had had a mind of its own . . .

THIRTY-FOUR

As Clint left his hotel the next morning he was practically accosted by Sheriff Hopkins.

"I want to talk to you, Adams!"

The lawman was still wearing the ridiculous Stetson he'd had the other night at the town meeting.

"Sheriff, I really do think you need a new hat. That one just doesn't—"

"Never mind my goddamned hat. What do you mean by getting my deputy drunk—"

"Sheriff, I really don't have time to talk to you right now—"

"Well, you'd better damn well make time," the sheriff said, poking his forefinger into Clint's chest.

"Sheriff . . . move your finger."

The two men exchanged glares until finally the sheriff lowered his eyes and removed his finger.

"I've got an appointment this morning, Sheriff, and when that's finished, I'll come over and talk to you in your office. That's a promise."

"I don't need your promises. Who do you have an appointment with?"

"Henry Deaver."

"Hah! The banker?" Clearly, the man didn't believe him. "Why would he want to see you?"

"Well, now, whether or not he wanted you to know that would be up to him, wouldn't it?"

"Why don't I just walk you over there to his house," Hopkins asked, with a knowing look on his face.

"Sure, come along."

The look on the lawman's face crumbled, but he blustered and said, "Let's go."

They walked to Deaver's little miniature mansion together without a word passing between them, and it was Hopkins who pounded on the door.

Deaver came out dressed for work in his banker's suit and was obviously surprised to see Hopkins there.

"Sheriff, what can I do for you?"

"This jasper was trying to tell me that he had an appointment with you this morning. I knew—"

"He does. It is a breakfast appointment and you are keeping us from it."

"Listen, Mr. Deaver, I have to talk with this man—"

"You can have him when I'm finished, Sheriff," Deaver said. He turned to Clint and said, "Shall we go?" and it was clearly a dismissal of the sheriff.

Which the lawman didn't like.

That was one more thing the sheriff could dislike Clint Adams for.

"We both have the same interests," Clint said to Henry Deaver over breakfast.

He had expected the banker to take him to the businessman's café, but instead he had led the way to a small café on a side street where the food was excellent, even better than at the hotel. If nothing else, Chalmers had its share of respectable eateries.

"You are correct about that, sir," Deaver said, lighting a large stogie. He apparently liked having a cigar with breakfast, and not after. "We do indeed have the same interests—if for somewhat different reasons."

Clint smiled.

"You mean that you care more about the killer ruining your chance for the train depot than you do that he—or she—is actually killing people."

TRIAL BY FIRE 143

"The train depot means very much to this town, Mr. Adams. It is not my personal welfare I am concerned with."

Clint knew that was so much bull crap. If the depot came through town, the town would grow, and if the town grew, Deaver's bank would also, possibly making him one of the wealthiest men in the state.

They had discussed the murders at length, and Clint had told Deaver about the notes that the sheriff had withheld from the newspapers.

"It's something I'm a little surprised he was smart enough to do," Clint said candidly.

"I see we have a similar opinion of our town's sheriff," Deaver said. "Perhaps it was the mayor's idea—but that seems even less likely."

"Did you read that report last night?"

"I did."

"And what do you think?"

"It sounds as if the man was writing a dime novel."

"I agree."

"Do you believe it to be accurate."

"Why would it be otherwise?"

"I believe that Mr. Greaves was a devious man, Mr. Adams. Why else would Alan Pinkerton have fired him?"

"Pinkerton fires men who don't smoke the same cigars as he does."

"You know Pinkerton?" Deaver asked in surprise.

"I do."

"Have you ever worked for him?"

"I've had offers."

"And turned them down."

Clint nodded.

"I see."

"Let's get back to the problem at hand, Mr. Deaver."

"What do you propose to do now that we know

who the murderess is? Tell the sheriff?"

"Unfortunately, Greaves's notes are not the proof the sheriff would need to make an arrest," Clint said quickly. He was actually thinking of his promise to Dr. Vernon.

"I could hire you."

"To do what?"

"Uh . . . take care of her. I know you by reputation, 'the Gunsmith' and all that. Isn't that what you do?"

"Are you asking me if I would kill her for money?" Clint asked, his anger barely restrained.

"Oh . . . of course not," Deaver said, recognizing the fact that he had an angry man at the table with him. "I was simply . . . inquiring as to what . . . what you would do next."

"Try to prove that she's the murderess, of course."

"How?"

"I don't know—yet."

"And what of Mr. Greaves, and . . . and that haberdasher?"

"They're not going anywhere. In fact, if their bodies aren't found, the woman in question might get nervous and make a mistake."

"I see. Uh . . . excuse me for asking this, but would you want a fee for what you are . . . doing?"

"I've been working on this all along without a fee, Mr. Deaver. I think I'll continue to do so."

"Just so we get that out of the way ahead of time," Deaver said.

"Don't worry, Mr. Banker. When this is over I won't come to you looking for money."

"Well, if you catch her, you would certainly be entitled to . . . to some sort of bonus." Deaver gestured with his cigar. "The bonus I was going to give Greaves."

"If this woman does turn out to be the murderer, then it will have been Greaves who did all the work."

"Alas, he is not alive to collect."

"Then you're getting off cheap."

Clint stood up, having lost his appetite from a combination of the banker's hot air and bad cigar.

"Where are you going?"

"I promised to go and talk to the sheriff."

"Do you have those notes you were mentioning?"

"I do," Clint said, touching his pocket.

"Perhaps it would not be wise of you to go to the sheriff's office with them. You would have to explain how you got them."

"You're right about that."

"I, on the other hand," Deaver said, "would not be obliged to explain." Deaver put his hand out and after a moment's thought Clint gave him the notes.

"There are three here," the banker said.

"I left Ogden's on his body."

"Ah, wise move." Deaver tucked the notes away in his jacket pocket. "If the sheriff should ask about the notes, simply tell him that I have them."

"All right."

"Mr. Adams—" Deaver said as Clint was walking away.

"Yes?"

"I have been a resident of this town since it was built. Railroad or no, I would like to see this killer brought to justice."

"So would I, Mr. Deaver. So would I."

THIRTY-FIVE

Clint went from the little restaurant to the sheriff's office and found Hopkins seated behind his desk.

"Finished with your little meeting?" the lawman asked.

"Yes. Now it's time for ours."

Clint pulled over a chair and sat in it.

"I didn't ask you to sit down."

Clint didn't answer.

"All right . . . what do you think you're doing?"

"I'm finding a killer. What have you been doing, besides inciting a mob—a lynch mob. Or, to be more precise, a burning mob."

"That doctor is weird, and this town doesn't have to put up with him and his crazies."

"He's trying to help those people."

"Then let him help them someplace else. While he's helping most of them, one of them is killing people in this town, and I don't like that."

"That's no justification for trying to burn him out."

"The first time we tried," Hopkins said, putting his feet down on the floor with a loud bang, "the next time we'll do it."

"If there is a next time."

"You a friend of his, or something?"

"Or something," Clint said. "The fact of the matter is I'm going to catch your killer, so there won't be any reason for you and your mob to burn him out."

"You think you know who the killer is?"

"I . . . have an idea."

"Then tell me and I'll arrest him. After all, that's my job."

"Is it? I didn't know you remembered what your job was supposed to be, Sheriff."

"I could also lock you up, Adams."

"For what?"

"For getting those notes from my deputy. Those notes are evidence, and you're tampering with 'em."

"What notes, Sheriff? I can't tamper with something I don't know anything about."

"Then why were you getting my deputy drunk?"

Clint shrugged.

"I bought the man a few drinks. How was I to know he couldn't hold his liquor?"

"You know about those notes, Adams. The ones from the so-called 'Phantom Lady'."

"Phantom Lady? Who is that?"

"That's the way the killer signed those notes to lure those men to their deaths. All of the men who were killed were between forty and fifty, and they all fancied themselves as ladies' men. That's why the killer was able to use those notes to get them out to Pierce Hollow—all except the third one, but he was probably on his way to Pierce Hollow when he was killed."

"I still don't know what notes—"

The sheriff slammed his big hand down on the desk, making a sound almost like a gunshot.

"You got that lamebrain Eugene drunk and he gave you the notes. I've got witnesses—"

"Produce them."

Hopkins frowned.

"Does Eugene say he gave me those notes?"

"Of course not."

"Then maybe you should talk to your banker."

TRIAL BY FIRE

"Mr. Deaver? Why?"

"He said something to me this morning about having some notes in his possession. Maybe you should go and lock him up, Sheriff."

"What I do about Mr. Deaver is my business, Adams. The sooner you and that detective fella understand that, the better off you'll both be."

"Detective fella?"

"Greaves, the ex-Pinkerton Deaver hired to embarrass me. He figured if he could get an outsider in here to catch the killer, he'd be able to put up a candidate to take my job at the next election."

"From what I saw at that meeting the other night, you seem to have a large part of the voting populace pretty securely in your pocket."

"That would change in an instant if I don't catch that killer."

"Or if you went *against* that hanging mob when they headed out to the Vernon institute.

"You were a lawman for a lot of years, Adams. You know what it's like to try and keep your job."

Clint couldn't believe it. Hopkins was trying to appeal to him as a spiritual brother, lawman to lawman.

"I walked away from the job for just that reason, Hopkins."

"Yeah, well, I ain't walking away from this one. They're gonna have to vote me out."

Clint thought a moment.

"You say that Deaver has a candidate he wants to put into office instead of you?"

"Not anybody specific, but whoever he puts in would report directly to him."

"And you don't?"

"I been the sheriff here for twelve years, Adams, and I been butting heads with Deaver every month of every year. No, I'm not in his pocket."

"What about the mayor?"

"The mayor stumbled into office when Deaver's candidate died of a heart attack during his campaigning."

"And you sort of led him around?"

"He leans on me, yeah."

Clint wondered if the town would be any worse off with somebody that Deaver put into office. Then again, he had seen towns where the law reported to one man, and it wouldn't be long before Chalmers would undergo a name change and be called "Deavertown."

"I'll tell you what, Sheriff."

"What?"

"You keep your mob under control, and when I catch this killer I'll turn him over to you. You can take full credit for catching him—or her."

Hopkins frowned and studied Clint.

"Why would you do that?"

"I'll do it on one condition."

"What's that?"

"That you bring in a Federal marshal and turn the killer over to him."

Hopkins thought about that, rubbing his hand over his face, and then nodded.

"All right, I go along with you."

"Good. If you're going along with me, then get yourself a man you trust and a buckboard and be ready to ride out of here in a half an hour."

"Where to?"

"You'll know when we get there, Sheriff. Don't worry. You won't be disappointed."

Clint stood up and walked to the door.

"Hey, Adams?"

"What?"

TRIAL BY FIRE

"Why are you doing this?"

Clint shrugged.

"Like you said, Sheriff. I was a lawman for a lot of years. I know what it's like."

THIRTY-SIX

Eugene.

The man Sheriff Hopkins chose as the man he could trust was the deputy, Eugene.

Clint stared at Eugene, and then at Hopkins, who was sitting astride his horse right next to him.

"Eugene?" Clint asked.

"When he's sober, he's trustworthy," Hopkins said. "Besides, he's my nephew."

"Where we goin'?" Eugene called out.

Clint looked at Eugene and said, "We're going to Pierce Hollow, Eugene."

"Pierce Hollow?" the sheriff asked, giving Clint a funny look.

Clint nodded.

"Pierce Hollow."

They told Eugene to wait outside and then Clint led to the way to the cabin.

"Jesus Christ," Hopkins said when they entered. He loomed at Clint and asked, "When?"

"Late last night."

"Who are they?"

"Take a look."

Hopkins walked over and took a closer look at the bodies.

"This is the detective, Greaves, and the other one . . . that's Ogden, the haberdasher."

"Right."

"You knew about this?"

"I found Greaves when I was . . . out riding."

"Out riding . . . at night?"

Clint ignored the remark.

"After that, I found Ogden in here. I pulled Greaves inside to keep him away from the animals."

"Why didn't you tell me?" Hopkins demanded, facing Clint. Clint felt that whatever spirit of cooperation they had established in the sheriff's office was in danger of going right out the window.

"What did you want me to do, wake you up last night and tell you I found two bodies? They weren't going anywhere. I was going to tell you this morning, but then you braced me at the hotel. I figured I'd tell you after I spoke to Deaver, and after you . . . cooled down."

Hopkins glared at Clint, then turned and looked down at the two men.

"I guess they weren't going anywhere," he said. Any trace of belligerence in his tone had gone. "Why didn't you tell me in town?"

"I just wanted you and one other man—Eugene— out here, not a whole mob. This has got to be kept quiet, Sheriff, if we're going to catch the killer tonight."

"I understand."

"Do you? If word of this doesn't get around, it might hurt the killer's ego. He might make a mistake."

"And he might kill somebody else, just out of spite."

Clint had to admit that was a possibility, but since he had a pretty good idea who the killer was, he thought he could keep an eye on her.

"That's a chance we'll have to take if we want to catch him."

Hopkins thought that over and said, "All right. We'll load the bodies onto a buckboard and bring them into town by a back road." He turned to face

Clint and said, "You know, if you *had* woke me up last night we could have taken them into town in the dark."

Damned if Hopkins didn't have a point there.

They got the bodies into town and to the undertaker's without anyone noticing.

"What do we do now?" Hopkins asked.

"The next step is one I have to take myself, Sheriff," Clint said, "but I promise to bring you into it as soon as possible."

"Wait a minute," Hopkins said, "I thought we were cooperating here."

"We are, but—"

"You're going after the killer alone."

"Sheriff, I'm going after the person I *think* is the killer. If I'm wrong, I don't want you or some trigger-happy deputy or posse member to shoot . . . him. I've got to be sure about this."

Hopkins digested this and then backed off.

"All right, all right, I'll keep going along with you a little longer."

Clint left, having the feeling that at a moment's notice he could lose the sheriff back to the mob.

THIRTY-SEVEN

There was something about his meeting with Louise Hanratty that stuck in Clint Adams's mind. It went beyond the fact that the woman had a doll-like beauty that was certainly memorable. It had more to do with the fact that when he met her she was beating a man over the head with an umbrella.

It was the umbrella—thanks to R. D. Greaves's written report—that stuck in Clint's mind.

Still, in spite of what was written in the report, he had to see some evidence for himself before condemning anyone.

Louise lived on the second floor of a boardinghouse which Clint had not checked out yet. He knew, however, from Greaves's report, that her window was in the back of the building, second from the left as you faced it.

Clint did not know how Greaves had gotten into the room—that much had not been in the report—but the town had not awakened and many of the townspeople were on their way to work, or to whatever it was they did during the day.

Clint went to the rear of the boardinghouse and, hoping that most of the boarders had gone, forced the back door and went up the back steps. He reached Louise Hanratty's door without being noticed, but now the question was: Where was she? Inside, or gone?

He listened intently at the door and heard nothing.

He put his hand on the doorknob.

He turned it slowly.

The door opened and he went in.

The bed was neatly made. The surface of the chest of drawers was uncluttered.

The place was empty.

He spent the next few minutes looking around.

Not until he reached behind the shawl-draped rocking chair did he find the umbrella.

He picked it up, examined it, and eventually figured out how to open it. It came apart in his hands, and he eased the blade out.

The handle was still damp from where it had been washed, but as carefully as the blade might have been cleaned, there were still traces of dry blood on it.

He went over to the bureau and looked into the washbowl.

Nothing.

Then he got an idea. He picked up the pitcher and poured the water into the bowl.

It poured out a brackish red.

Blood red.

He saw what she had done. She had cleaned off the handle and the blade and then poured the water back into the pitcher until she could dispose of it.

He let himself out as quietly as he had entered.

He had to find Louise Hanratty.

The undertaker, a man named Forest, stared down at the bodies of both Ogden and Greaves. Both had obviously been killed by the same person who killed the other three.

The killer had struck again.

The sheriff was obviously trying to keep this a secret, but Forest's tongue burned to be wagging.

Maybe if he told just one person?

What kind of harm could that do?

Louise had apparently disappeared.

He searched for a good part of the day, and as early evening approached he figured he was going to have to go to Hopkins now and tell him everything.

As he approached the man's office, though, he saw them.

The mob.

About thirty angry people, most of them men, gathered in front of the sheriff's office.

Somehow, the word had gotten out.

He found a doorway and settled in to watch, and listen. This would tell him just how much he could rely on the sheriff.

THIRTY-EIGHT

"We burned 'em out once, and we can do it again—this time for good," one of the people cried out.

They were waiting for the sheriff and the mayor to make an official appearance, now that it had been confirmed that two more bodies had been found.

From inside his office both Hopkins and the mayor could hear the crowd.

"Well, what do you plan to do?" the mayor demanded.

"I told you. I'm waiting for Adams—"

"Is Adams going to help you subdue this mob? He's working for Vernon, you told me that yourself after the meeting. Have you changed your mind?"

"Maybe I was wrong—"

"And maybe you weren't. Maybe he's just trying to give Vernon time to escape."

"I never said I thought Vernon did the killings."

"No, you said that one of his crazies had done them. As far as I'm concerned, it amounts to the same thing."

From outside they heard something strike the door.

"Hopkins, do you want them to lynch us?" the mayor demanded.

It irked Hopkins to have the mayor talking to him this way. He was the one who the mayor usually relied on for decisions. It was he who usually spoke to the mayor in this tone, and not the other way around.

Had he been wrong about Adams? After all, the man *had* hidden from him the fact that two more murders had been committed.

Was he giving Vernon time to get himself and his crazies away?

Maybe it wouldn't hurt just to go out there and find out.

"All right," Hopkins said, "all right, let's talk to them."

As they stepped outside, the crowd quieted down expectantly.

"I know why you're all here," Hopkins called out. "I guess I might as well confirm what you've heard. Two more men were killed in the same manner as the others."

"When?" somebody shouted.

"It happened last night."

"And you know damn well who done it!" someone shouted.

The mayor raised a pudgy hand and shouted, "I've talked this over with the sheriff and I'm still arguing on the side of justice instead of lynch law."

With that statement he considered that he had secured his office for next term. People liked a mayor who stood for law and order—even if they were a mob.

A man stepped forward and called out, "How do you feel about this, Sheriff?"

"I don't condone hanging," Hopkins said, "or burning, but I think it might be a good idea for us to go out and just ask Dr. Vernon a few questions."

A cheer went up from the crowd and in his doorway the Gunsmith felt a shiver run up and down his spine.

The mob and the sheriff certainly had two different things in mind.

THIRTY-NINE

Clint rushed away from the scene and hurried to Amy Todd's house. He intended to tell Amy everything, that he knew that she and Delores and Louise had all walked away from Dr. Vernon's institute. He was hoping to enlist her aide—and Delores's, as well—in finding Louise and talking her into giving herself up. Hopefully, they'd be able to head the mob off before more violence erupted.

He reached the house and knocked on the door.

After a few moments he knocked again.

Nothing.

He walked around the house and peered through the window of her bedroom. She wasn't there. He went to the back of the house and knocked on the back door.

No answer.

He tried the doorknob and found the door locked. The lock was flimsy, so he pressed his weight against the door and forced it open.

He went through the house and did not find a sign of Amy Todd. He had also thought that perhaps Louise had gone to Amy or Delores for help, but there was no sign that either woman had been there over the past few hours.

He turned to leave when his eyes fell on the umbrella where he had seen it before.

An umbrella.

It couldn't be.

He'd already found the blade hidden in Louise's

umbrella. There was no reason to check Amy's.

No reason at all.

He walked over and picked up the umbrella. It was the same one, and it came apart in his hands the same way. There was dried blood on it.

Jesus, he thought. Oh, Jesus.

Both of them?

He dropped the umbrella and hurried to the back door, to go out the way he had come in.

Greaves's report had revealed how he had entered Louise Hanratty's room and found the blade in the umbrella. Obviously, after that Greaves had looked no further.

Now that Clint had found the same blade and umbrella in Amy Todd's room, what was the answer?

Was one a killer, or both?

And if it was both of them, why?

Unless . . .

As he opened the back door to leave, a bullet went past his head and slammed into the wood of the door.

He went into a crouch and rolled forward, away from the porch and behind a huge rain barrel.

He knelt there, waiting for a second shot so he could pinpoint the direction the first had come from.

Finally, he decided that the next move would have to be his if he wasn't going to stay crouched there all night.

He started around the rain barrel when a most unlikely occurrence took place.

The man who had shot at him stood up.

Straight up.

Right there in the open.

Tall and proud.

So that any half-blind barfly with a gun could have blown his head off, especially since the badge on his chest made such a good target.

TRIAL BY FIRE

"I'm arrestin' you in the name of the law!" the man shouted.

"Eugene, you ass," Clint called out. "Is that you?"

"Aw, hell, Clint. Is that you?"

"Hell, yes, it's me, you dummy."

Clint stood up, his knees cracking as he did.

"I was walkin' by when I saw someone moving around by the house. I thought it was a thief."

"Come over here."

Eugene hurried over, holstering his gun.

"Do you know where my room is?"

"Yeah, sure."

"There's a book in my room, on the table near my bed."

"A book?"

"Yes, a book with a red cover."

"There's a mob forming, Clint, and you wanna read a book—?"

"No, no—listen to me. Do you know a red-haired woman named Delores, takes tickets at the theater?"

"I sure do."

"I need you to get me that book and meet me at her place as soon as you can. Can you do that?"

"Sure I can. I'm a deputy, ain't I?"

"Right, you're a deputy."

Eugene started to run away when Clint called out, "Eugene!"

"What?" the deputy asked.

"Do you know where Delores lives?"

"Uh . . . no," he replied sheepishly.

Clint sighed and said, "Well, come back here and I'll tell you."

FORTY

It took time for the mob to get mounted and meet back at the sheriff's office. The women who wanted to accompany the men were also mounted, or had fetched their buckboards and buggies.

It was dark now, and although the torches that many of the men were carrying could have been used simply to light the way, there were those who had other uses in mind for them.

The sheriff, mounted himself, called out his orders.

"Remember now I expect each and every one of you to act only on my orders."

"Sure, Sheriff."

"Dr. Vernon's got legal rights, and I expect you to respect them."

"We'll show him respect," someone shouted.

"Yeah," someone else called out, "right after we show him some firepower."

"Fire," of course, being the operative word.

Delores lived on the second floor of a small, but classier boardinghouse than Louise did. Stairs for a separate entrance to the second floor ran along the side of the house. Windows in the front were lit as people were looking out, interest aroused by the mob. There was only one room in the back that was lit, however.

Clint skirted some trash barrels and went up the stairs quietly. He moved along the balcony until he reached the rear, lighted window. If what he was thinking—what he had been thinking since discovering Amy's umbrella—was true, then he was better off approaching silently.

As he reached the window he pressed himself against the wall to listen. It soon became obvious that all three women were present in the room.

Maybe his theory wasn't so farfetched, after all.

"You must admit it, Louise," Delores said sternly. "You killed the two of them tonight."

He took a chance and peered in the window.

Delores of the red hair and Amy, with her silver-streaked dark hair, stood over Louise Hanratty, who was sitting in a straight-backed chair between them, shoulders slumped.

"I—" Louise began, but she couldn't complete her sentence. Instead, she broke into uncontrollable tears.

Clint's eyes swept the room and he finally spotted it, leaning against the wall. A third umbrella, exactly like the other two.

"We're trying to help you," Amy Todd said in her soft librarian's voice.

She knelt next to her friend Louise and embraced her.

"Everything will be all right. You'll see."

"B-but I killed a man," Louise sobbed.

Delores said, "So did I."

"And I," Amy said.

Suddenly at the bottom of the steps, there was a thunderous racket, as if someone had stumbled into the trash barrels.

No need to guess who it was.

"Eugene," Clint said under his breath.

At the sound of the noise, Delores picked up a rifle from a table and looked to the window.

"You bastard!" she shouted at Clint, leveling the weapon at him, "you were listening all along."

FORTY-ONE

By the time the mob reached Dr. Vernon's institute, many of the riders had dropped their torches along the roadside, preferring to fill their hands with weapons.

"I'm going to call his name," Hopkins called out. "You men give him a chance."

"A chance to do what?" someone asked.

"A chance to confess before we hang 'im!" another shouted.

By now, the sheriff was caught up in all this, as well. He'd felt all along that Vernon was behind this. Whatever Clint Adams thought, when Vernon was dead, the killings would stop.

Dr. Vernon thought he might have made a mistake about Clint Adams. The thing that started him thinking that was when Adams took the book on Franz Mesmer.

Still, Adams was the least of his worries now, as he heard the sounds of the mob outside.

He had no doubt what they wanted, and he was a fool to have given them a second chance at him.

This time he might not escape.

"Dr. Vernon?"

He turned and saw the housekeeper standing there, a rifle in her hands.

"You will need this, sir."

She was so grave that he almost laughed. What good would the rifle do against a mob? Now, if he had enough rifles to arm all of the patients, and enough time to prepare them . . .

"Thank you," Vernon said, accepting the rifle.

It was all he could do, for now.

Delores had gotten too close to the window to get a shot at Clint, and he had reached in, grasped the rifle by the barrel, and pulled it out of her hand. After that he had climbed in the window, followed closely by Eugene, who tripped and fell on his face.

Despite themselves, the three women had laughed.

Which was a good sign.

He convinced them to listen as he read from Franz Mesmer's book. It was the one thing he remembered from the book, before setting it aside. The one thing he understood.

When he was finished Delores spoke first.

"My God."

Louise began sobbing again.

"That's horrid!" Amy Todd said.

"What have we done?" Louise cried into her hands.

Eugene looked hopelessly confused.

"You haven't done anything, Louise," Clint said. "Oh, practically speaking you have, but it wasn't honestly your doing. It was Dr. Vernon."

Delores went over to where the umbrella was, picked it up, and promptly threw it out of the window.

"I don't want that in my room!"

"What will happen to us?" Amy asked. She was crouched next to Louise, holding her shoulders.

"I can't say for sure," Clint said. "I'd have to talk to the sheriff, maybe to a judge, but right now Eugene and I have something else to do."

"*We* do?" Eugene asked.

"Yes, Eugene, we. We've got to stop a mob."

"But why? You just said he was guilty."

"I know," Clint said, not feeling very proud of himself. He had, after all, been taken in by the doctor, while the people who made up the mob had been right. "Still, we can't let the mob kill him. He's got to stand trial. And there are other patients in that institute who are innocent victims. They might die, as well, unless we stop them."

"I can't see how much help I'd be to you," Eugene said, "being so clumsy and all."

The wrong time for Eugene to start to realize that, Clint thought.

"You can be my decoy."

"Decoy."

"Sure. You ride on ahead of me so that if they open fire, they'll be gunning for you, first."

"Yer funnin' me, ain't you, Clint?" Eugene asked hopefully.

"Yes, Eugene, I'm funning you. Are you coming?"

"I don't know why," Eugene said, "but I'm comin'."

FORTY-TWO

Hopkins lost control right from the start.

When Vernon didn't answer his call, several of the men from the mob stormed the front door. Others rode around to find other entry.

Several men smashed a window on the east end of the institute and climbed in. Once they had gained entrance, the rest of their mission was easy to accomplish.

They slashed and kicked over furniture, forced open doors to allow the patients to run free.

Two of them kicked in a door and found a lovely woman of about thirty. Having been awakened, she was sitting naked in bed, staring at them. They both stared at her firm breasts and then one man licked his lips.

"Hey," he told his friend, "shut the door, huh?"

He pulled the woman from the bed and pushed her down to her knees . . .

Among some of the patients were some extremely deformed people. All sorts of sorrowful sights confronted the mob. Other windows were broken, and when the front gate was opened from the inside, total access had been gained.

Some of the men had brought whiskey bottles with them and had been passing them around during the ride to the institute. Now liquored up and convinced they were doing God's will, they herded patients into the main room, teased them, tore off their clothes, and tried to see how badly they could frighten them.

By the time the sheriff entered the building, the place resembled something Sherman had left in his wake.

Hopkins went looking for Dr. Vernon.

Wandering the halls he heard pitiful screams coming from behind closed doors. Behind one door he heard a woman screaming and a man shouting and could guess what was going on.

The longer it took him to find Vernon, the angrier he got, and the angrier he got the more he convinced himself that Vernon was behind the killings. Clint Adams was full of shit, and probably *was* working for Vernon.

Somewhere in the house a fire had started. He could smell the smoke, but he continued to search for Vernon.

He finally found the doctor in an upstairs room, stuffing clothing into a carpetbag.

"Vernon!" he shouted.

The doctor turned and faced the sheriff, who had drawn his gun.

"You're finally going to pay for what you've done, Vernon," Hopkins said. "Finally."

As Clint and Eugene rode up to the institute they could hear the shouts from inside. Shouts from the mob and shouts from the patients.

From somewhere Clint could see smoke. He'd spotted many extinguished torches along the road on the way there, but obviously some of them had ended up inside the building.

"Are you going in there?" Eugene asked.

"Yes."

"Why?"

"To find the sheriff, and Dr. Vernon. To keep anyone else from being killed, I hope."

As he dismounted he saw some people come running

TRIAL BY FIRE

out the front gate. They were wearing night clothes and one man was even naked. They were obviously patients.

"Eugene, see if you can convince those people to stay close."

"How do I do that?"

"I don't know," Clint said. He simply did not want Eugene inside the building. "Talk to them. Maybe they'll listen."

Clint left Duke a safe distance from the building and ran through the front gate. Just inside the front door he caught a man abusing a female patient. She was about fifty and not attractive, but the man had pulled her robe open and was fondling her doughy breasts. He pulled the man away and the woman fled down the hall.

"Hey!" the man said.

Clint hit him, but held him up.

"Where's Hopkins?"

"I—I don't know. Whatcha hit me for?"

"Get out of here," Clint said, pushing the man out the door. "The deputy is out there. Help him keep the escaping patients close to the house."

"Hey, wait—"

"If I see you manhandling a patient again, I'll kill you. You understand that?"

"Yeah, yeah, I understand," the man said, and stumbled away, his mouth bleeding from the blow.

The smoke was thick on the first floor now, and people were yelling and running, patients and members of the mob alike. Clint grabbed one man from the mob and shouted the same instructions to him that he had given the other man. The man nodded, but he didn't know if he would obey.

He ran upstairs and saw that one of Dr. Vernon's staff was having trouble with the key to a door lock. Behind the door a patient was moaning.

"Let me try it."

The key was stuck.

He tried to turn it left, and then right, but he had no luck. The staff member was getting nervous now, and finally ran away, down the hall. Clint didn't bother calling after him. He concentrated on the lock. The smoke from downstairs was coiling up now, filling the upstairs hall.

He got down on his knees, where the smoke was not as bad, gritted his teeth, and turned the key with all his might, hoping it would not bend or break.

He heard the lock click, and the door opened.

A woman who must have been eighty stumbled out. She had stringy gray hair and was wearing a shabby robe.

"Thank you," she said.

"Can you make it downstairs?"

"Y-yes."

"Then get out of the house. There are others outside."

He started down the hall again, but stopped when he heard a woman screaming. She sounded as if she had been screaming for some time. He found the door where the screaming was coming from, and saw the broken lock.

He stepped inside.

A naked woman was on her knees while a man violated her from behind, driving into her as she screamed. A second man was watching, his eyes shiny, his pants down around his ankles. He had an erection, and although he had probably gone first, he was eagerly waiting for another chance.

"That's enough!" Clint shouted.

The man who was watching looked up and sneered.

"Get out of here."

Clint stepped into the man and kicked him hard in the balls. The man's eyes popped and he fell over, grabbing his wounded testicles.

The other man pulled away from the woman, a huge erection poking up from beneath a sloppy paunch.

"Don't kick me!"

Clint moved toward him and struck him in the face with his fist. The man staggered back, tripped on his pants, which were pooled around his feet, and fell.

"I should kill you," Clint said, helping the woman to her feet. She was crying, and he found her robe and passed it to her. "I should lock you in and let you burn."

"No, no," the man pleaded.

"Get dressed and take your friend out of here. I'll be looking for you later."

The man staggered to his feet, pulled his pants up, and reached for his friend.

"He can't stand," he complained.

Clint pushed the woman out the door, telling her to get out of the house.

"Drag him or carry him, but get out of this house," Clint told the man. "If I find out you've touched a woman again, I'll kill you both."

"I hear ya, mister, I hear ya," the man said, dragging his friend out the door.

Clint was off down the hall again, and through the last door he found Hopkins.

The lawman was sprawled through the doorway leading to Dr. Vernon's bedroom. Vernon stood there with a derringer in his right hand, the sort you might see come out of a gambler's sleeve.

"He tried to kill me, Clint," Vernon said. It did not escape the Gunsmith's notice that the man did not put the derringer down—and it *was* a two-shot derringer.

"Maybe you'll regret that he didn't."

"What are you talking about?"

"Franz Mesmer."

"What? Are you mad? What about Mesmer?"

"When we first met you told me all about Franz Mesmer."

The smoke started to infiltrate the room.

"Can we discuss this downstairs?" Vernon asked. "Outside?"

"No, right here. One of the things you told me was that Mesmer had been asked to stop his experiments with hypnosis."

"So, what's that got to do with anything?"

Clint shook his head.

"You bastard. You had me believing that you were an innocent victim. Those three women in town, they didn't escape. You sent them there."

"You *are* mad."

"You've been conducting the same kind of mind experiments that Mesmer was, controlling people's minds. You got those women to kill those men."

"You're insane, Adams."

"No, Doctor, I'm afraid you are. Insane, and arrogant. In your arrogance you stayed here after they burned you out the first time and continued your experiments. What did you think, Doctor, that you could control the whole town, eventually?"

"We have to get out of here, Adams," the doctor said.

Behind him, Clint could now hear the crackling of flames.

"Not until you admit what you are."

"We'll suffocate, or burn to death!"

"Those three women will hang unless you tell the truth, Doctor."

The smoke was becoming thick enough to bother both of their eyes. Clint started to cough and he knew what Vernon would do.

The doctor pulled the trigger, but in his haste and

TRIAL BY FIRE

with the rolling smoke, he missed. He threw the derringer at Clint and sprang at him. The derringer struck Clint just above the right eye, and then the doctor was on him. The man's thin build belied his strength, which Clint felt as Vernon's hand went around his throat.

Clint brought his knee up into Vernon's groin and the man's hold on his throat weakened. He broke the hold and punched the doctor in the face. With a satisfying crunch the doctor's nose broke, blood gushing forth over his lips.

Still on the floor Vernon slithered toward the door, trying to escape. Clint moved quickly and sat on the man's back. He reached forward, cupped his hand beneath the doctor's chin, and pulled up.

"We'll sit here and watch the fire reach us, Doctor."

"No, no," the man gurgled.

"Then talk to me."

"All right, all right. I hypnotized all three women and sent them into town to kill."

"Who?"

"It was up to them to choose the targets, but knowing all their pasts, I expected them to choose amoral men."

"Men who cheated on their wives, mistreated women?"

"Yes, yes. God, we've got to get out of here."

As Clint got up from the man's back he saw that he might have waited too long. The hallways were a mass of flames now.

"Get up!"

Vernon sprang to his feet and ran into the hallway.

"Not that way!" Clint shouted, but it was too late. The doctor's clothing caught fire and soon he was being consumed by the flames, as Whitfield had been consumed.

Clint started to move for the window when he heard a moan. He turned and saw the sheriff move his hand.

Hopkins was alive.

Clint bent over the man and turned him over onto his back. Hopkins's eyes fluttered open.

"Did you hear all that?" Clint asked.

"I . . . heard."

"Then let's get out of here."

Clint lifted the lawman up on his shoulder and carried him toward the window, marveling at how this adventure was ending just exactly as it had begun.

FORTY-THREE

" 'The steps leading to the Lord's House' " Delores said a week later.

It had taken almost a week to get a judge to Chalmers. While Hopkins was laid up, Eugene was acting sheriff, but he relied heavily on Clint's advice.

The women were held, but instead of holding them in cells they were each given a room at the hotel. When the judge arrived, a hearing was held, where all the evidence was presented. With the testimony of Sheriff Hopkins, who struggled out of bed in order to testify in person, the judge decided that none of the women were at fault for what they did.

"The Lord's House isn't too hard to figure," Delores said.

She was standing in front of the church with Clint, Amy Todd, Louise Hanratty, and the mayor, who had given his permission for the steps to be torn up so they could dig, if necessary.

Clint had decided not to tell anyone—especially Delores—that the diamonds her father had left her were stolen. He did not show her the letter. He told her that her father's last words had been of his love for her, and of the steps to the Lord's House.

Delores turned to the other two women and held out her hands for them to take.

"We've become very good friends, girls."

"Yes we have," Amy said.

"Indeed," Louise said.

The histories of the three women that Clint had received from Dr. Vernon were false. The women did all at one time have emotional problems, and to his credit Dr. Vernon did help them—until the time he decided to use them for his experiments.

All of Dr. Vernon's other patients had been transferred to other hospitals to undergo tests.

Clint smiled, knowing what Delores was going to say.

"Anything we find below these steps," Delores said, "is going to be shared among the three of us."

The women all laughed, and embraced.

It took half an hour to take the steps apart, and then Clint sent the workmen away and did the digging himself.

Twenty minutes later Clint stopped digging, reached down, and retrieved a small leather satchel.

He brought it up, dusted red dirt from it, and opened it.

What was inside sparkled like the stars dotting the night sky.

"Good Lord!" breathed Delores.

"I would say that this calls for a celebration," the mayor said as Clint climbed up out of the hole. He had remained as an observer. "We should all repair to the hotel for some good food and wine."

"Begging your pardon, Mayor," Delores said, casting conspiratorial glances at the other two women, "but that isn't the sort of celebration we had in mind—is it, girls?"

"No," Louise said.

"No," Amy said, as all girls looked at Clint, "not at all."

An hour later, freshly bathed, Clint lay between a

TRIAL BY FIRE

redhead and a raven-haired lass with a silver streak in her hair—and a doll-like blonde seated at the base of the bed.

Everyone was naked, and passing around a communal bottle of champagne.

"What will you ladies do now?" Clint asked.

"Well, since you saved us all from the gallows by getting that confession from Dr. Vernon," Delores said, "we thought we'd leave Chalmers and set up some kind of business somewhere with the diamonds my father left me."

"What kind of business?"

"We haven't decided yet," Delores said.

"Maybe we'll open a cathouse," Amy said.

Louise blushed, but kept staring at the tent Clint had made out of the sheet between his legs. Lying here with three beautiful women—all naked—how could he not be the proud owner of a . . . an eager erection.

"Why leave Chalmers?" he asked.

"That's best, Clint," Delores said. "Even if we were being controlled by Vernon, we did kill some people."

"The people in this town will sooner or later remember that," Amy said.

"Then I guess you're right," Clint said. "When will you be leaving?"

"Oh, not until we've adequately repaid you for saving us," Delores said.

"And we certainly intend to repay you in our own special way," Amy Todd said.

Louise nodded anxiously, having some time ago lost her prim and proper countenance. Clint thought it might have been as soon as they stripped off her clothes, which had come after a few pulls on the champagne bottle. She had the smallest breasts of the three women—and the only set he had not yet seen—but they were equally firm and lovely.

"Well now, how would you all be intending to do that?"

Delores leaned against him, pressing her breasts against his chest as Amy told Louise, "Show him, Louise."

With that Louise snatched the sheet away from him so that his erection bobbed free. Amy was pressing against his other side while Louise slid up between his legs, reaching shyly, but surely . . .

"Champagne, anyone?" he asked.

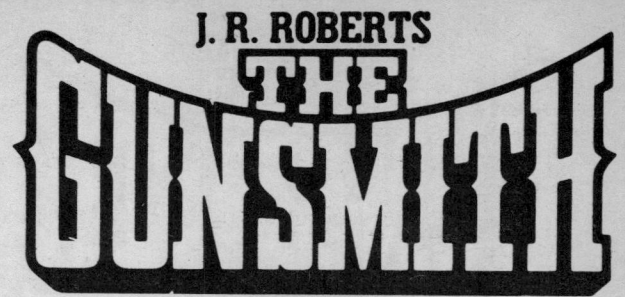

J. R. ROBERTS
THE GUNSMITH
SERIES

☐ 30932-1	THE GUNSMITH #1:	MACKLIN'S WOMEN	$2.50
☐ 30930-5	THE GUNSMITH #7:	THE LONGHORN WAR	$2.50
☐ 30923-2	THE GUNSMITH #9:	HEAVYWEIGHT GUN	$2.50
☐ 30924-0	THE GUNSMITH #10:	NEW ORLEANS FIRE	$2.50
☐ 30931-3	THE GUNSMITH #11:	ONE-HANDED GUN	$2.50
☐ 30926-7	THE GUNSMITH #12:	THE CANADIAN PAYROLL	$2.50
☐ 30868-6	THE GUNSMITH #13:	DRAW TO AN INSIDE DEATH	$2.50
☐ 30922-4	THE GUNSMITH #14:	DEAD MAN'S HAND	$2.50
☐ 30905-4	THE GUNSMITH #15:	BANDIT GOLD	$2.50
☐ 30907-0	THE GUNSMITH #17:	SILVER WAR	$2.25
☐ 30908-9	THE GUNSMITH #18:	HIGH NOON AT LANCASTER	$2.50
☐ 30909-7	THE GUNSMITH #19:	BANDIDO BLOOD	$2.50
☐ 30929-1	THE GUNSMITH #20:	THE DODGE CITY GANG	$2.50
☐ 30910-0	THE GUNSMITH #21:	SASQUATCH HUNT	$2.50
☐ 30895-3	THE GUNSMITH #24:	KILLER GRIZZLY	$2.50
☐ 30897-X	THE GUNSMITH #26:	EAGLE'S GAP	$2.50
☐ 30902-X	THE GUNSMITH #29:	WILDCAT ROUND-UP	$2.50
☐ 30903-8	THE GUNSMITH #30:	THE PONDEROSA WAR	$2.50
☐ 30913-5	THE GUNSMITH #34:	NIGHT OF THE GILA	$2.50
☐ 30915-1	THE GUNSMITH #36:	BLACK PEARL SALOON	$2.50
☐ 30940-2	THE GUNSMITH #39:	THE EL PASO SALT WAR	$2.50
☐ 30941-0	THE GUNSMITH #40:	THE TEN PINES KILLER	$2.50
☐ 30942-9	THE GUNSMITH #41:	HELL WITH A PISTOL	$2.50

Available at your local bookstore or return this form to:

CHARTER
THE BERKLEY PUBLISHING GROUP, Dept. B
390 Murray Hill Parkway, East Rutherford, NJ 07073

Please send me the titles checked above. I enclose _____. Include $1.00 for postage and handling if one book is ordered; add 25¢ per book for two or more not to exceed $1.75. CA, NJ, NY and PA residents please add sales tax. Prices subject to change without notice and may be higher in Canada. Do not send cash.

NAME_____

ADDRESS_____

CITY_____ STATE/ZIP_____

(Allow six weeks for delivery.)

J. R. ROBERTS
THE GUNSMITH
SERIES

☐ 0-441-30952-6	THE GUNSMITH #48: ARCHER'S REVENGE	$2.50
☐ 0-441-30953-4	THE GUNSMITH #49: SHOWDOWN IN RATON	$2.50
☐ 0-441-30955-0	THE GUNSMITH #51: DESERT HELL	$2.50
☐ 0-441-30956-9	THE GUNSMITH #52: THE DIAMOND GUN	$2.50
☐ 0-441-30957-7	THE GUNSMITH #53: DENVER DUO	$2.50
☐ 0-441-30958-5	THE GUNSMITH #54: HELL ON WHEELS	$2.50
☐ 0-441-30959-3	THE GUNSMITH #55: THE LEGEND MAKER	$2.50
☐ 0-441-30961-5	THE GUNSMITH #57: CROSSFIRE MOUNTAIN	$2.50
☐ 0-441-30962-3	THE GUNSMITH #58: THE DEADLY HEALER	$2.50
☐ 0-441-30964-X	THE GUNSMITH #60: GERONIMO'S TRAIL	$2.50
☐ 0-441-30965-8	THE GUNSMITH #61: THE COMSTOCK GOLD FRAUD	$2.50
☐ 0-441-30966-6	THE GUNSMITH #62: BOOM TOWN KILLER	$2.50
☐ 0-441-30967-4	THE GUNSMITH #63: TEXAS TRACKDOWN	$2.50
☐ 0-441-30968-2	THE GUNSMITH #64: THE FAST DRAW LEAGUE	$2.50
☐ 0-441-30969-0	THE GUNSMITH #65: SHOWDOWN IN RIO MALO	$2.50
☐ 0-441-30970-4	THE GUNSMITH #66: OUTLAW TRAIL	$2.75
☐ 0-515-09058-1	THE GUNSMITH #67: HOMESTEADER GUNS	$2.75
☐ 0-515-09118-9	THE GUNSMITH #68: FIVE CARD DEATH	$2.75
☐ 0-515-09176-6	THE GUNSMITH #69: TRAIL DRIVE TO MONTANA	$2.75
☐ 0-515-09258-4	THE GUNSMITH #70: TRIAL BY FIRE	$2.75
☐ 0-515-09217-7	THE GUNSMITH #71: THE OLD WHISTLER GANG (on sale November '87)	$2.75

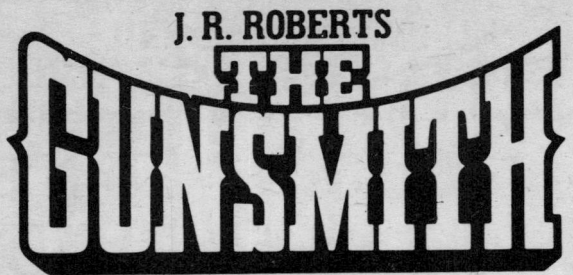

Please send the titles I've checked above. Mail orders to:

BERKLEY PUBLISHING GROUP
390 Murray Hill Pkwy., Dept. B
East Rutherford, NJ 07073

NAME_____

ADDRESS_____

CITY_____

STATE_____ ZIP_____

Please allow 6 weeks for delivery.
Prices are subject to change without notice.

POSTAGE & HANDLING:
$1.00 for one book, $.25 for each additional. Do not exceed $3.50.

BOOK TOTAL	$_____
SHIPPING & HANDLING	$_____
APPLICABLE SALES TAX (CA, NJ, NY, PA)	$_____
TOTAL AMOUNT DUE PAYABLE IN US FUNDS. (No cash orders accepted.)	$_____

MEET STRINGER MacKAIL
NEWSMAN, GUNMAN, LADIES' MAN.

LOU CAMERON'S
STRINGER

*"STRINGER's the hardest ridin',
hardest fightin' and hardest lovin' hombre
I've had the pleasure of encountering
in quite a while."*
—Tabor Evans, author of the LONGARM series

It's the dawn of the twentieth century
and the Old West is drawing to a close.
But for Stringer MacKail, the tough-skinned
reporter who is as handy with a .38 as he is
with the women, the shooting's just begun.

_0-441-79064-X	STRINGER	$2.75
_0-441-79022-4	STRINGER ON DEAD MAN'S RANGE #2	$2.75

Available at your local bookstore or return this form to:

CHARTER
THE BERKLEY PUBLISHING GROUP, Dept. B
390 Murray Hill Parkway, East Rutherford, NJ 07073

Please send me the titles checked above. I enclose _____. Include $1.00 for postage and handling if one book is ordered; add 25¢ per book for two or more not to exceed $1.75. CA, NJ, NY and PA residents please add sales tax. Prices subject to change without notice and may be higher in Canada. Do not send cash.

NAME_____

ADDRESS_____

CITY_____ STATE/ZIP_____

(Allow six weeks for delivery.)

The hard-hitting, gun-slinging Pride of the Pinkertons is riding solo in this new action-packed series.

J.D. HARDIN'S RAIDER

Sharpshooting Pinkertons Doc and Raider are legends in their own time, taking care of outlaws that the local sheriffs can't handle. Doc has decided to settle down and now Raider takes on the nastiest vermin the Old West has to offer single-handedly...charming the ladies along the way

_0-425-10348-X	**RAIDER: THE YUMA ROUNDUP #3**	$2.75
_0-425-10432-X	**RAIDER THE GUNS OF EL DORADO #4**	$2.75
_0-425-10519-9	**RAIDER THIRST FOR VENGEANCE #5** (On Sale November 1987)	$2.75

Please send the titles I've checked above. Mail orders to:

BERKLEY PUBLISHING GROUP
390 Murray Hill Pkwy., Dept. B
East Rutherford, NJ 07073

NAME_____
ADDRESS_____
CITY_____
STATE_____ ZIP_____

Please allow 6 weeks for delivery.
Prices are subject to change without notice.

POSTAGE & HANDLING:
$1.00 for one book, $.25 for each additional. Do not exceed $3.50.

BOOK TOTAL $____
SHIPPING & HANDLING $____
APPLICABLE SALES TAX (CA, NJ, NY, PA) $____
TOTAL AMOUNT DUE $____
PAYABLE IN US FUNDS.
(No cash orders accepted.)